ADORABLE FAT GIRL & THE SIX-WEEK TRANSFORMATION

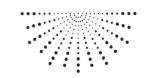

BERNICE BLOOM

DEAR READERS

Thanks so much for buying the latest adventure in the life of Mary Brown. This book can be read as a stand-alone book, or as part of the series of tales.

If you haven't read the others, here's a quick summary of Mary Brown's life to date. Thanks again everyone. Your support means so much to me. xxx

The story so far...

The first book opened with Mary Brown - our overweight heroine - deciding that she really needed to lose weight. She'd tried every diet under the sun, so it was time for a new approach...she headed down to 'Fat Club' where she met a whole load of new friends, and a man, called Ted, who she was really attracted to.

The first three books followed Mary's Fat Club experiences, and her growing admiration for Ted.

After that, we're into all the trips and adventures...and there are quite a few of them. The adventures start when Mary bumps into Dawn, an old school friend, who now runs a blog called 'Two Fat Ladies'. Dawn invites Mary to come on some trips with her, in return for Mary writing about them. The arrangement sees Mary go on a safari, on a cruise, and on a weight loss camp. Mary also heads to a yoga retreat and gets embroiled in an incredible mystery when she's invited to the funeral of someone she's never before (just she and five other people are invited, by the stranger on his deathbed...none of them has ever heard of the deceased. Why are they there?).

Mary's relationship with Ted is a bit up and down, and when they finally end it, her friends Charlie and Juan Pedro (an extravagant Spanish dancer who she met on the cruise and has come over to England to stay for a while) put her onto an internet dating site. Her experiences are chronicled in the last book (Adorable Fat Girl goes online dating).

So, that brings us to the present day. Mary is single. She hasn't seen Ted for months and is at home with Charlie, Dave (the gorgeous bloke who lives downstairs) and Juan.

They are sipping wine and chatting, when Mary makes a confession...

I hope you enjoy the book.

www.bernicebloom.com

CHAPTER ONE

"*I* am in love."

There. I finally said it. I had been feeling it for a long time, but it had taken a considerable amount of guts (and much gin) to brace myself enough to utter the words publicly.

I looked around the room at my friends: Dave, Charlie and Juan Pedro. They looked back at me with raised eyebrows, heads tilted to the side and knowing looks on their faces.

"Now tell us something we didn't know," said Charlie. "Because it's been obvious to all of us for some time that you're still head over heels in love with Ted."

I nodded solemnly. Anyone who has followed my adventures over the past few years will know that Ted is the love of my life. My joy. My kindred spirit. He brought warmth and colour to my days, made me happy and excited about the future, safe and comfortable. Any man capable of making you feel both excited and safe is a keeper. Even I know that.

So, I'm sure you're wondering...why aren't you with him then, Mary, you big dope?

The answer, dear friends, is because I managed to cock it all up. I just got a bit bored with the relationship and let it drift away, and he got bored, too, and let it drift further away. Then I felt like he wasn't trying to keep us together and I called it off completely and that was that.

"I've tried not to be in love with him," I said to my little audience. "I've tried really hard. But I just can't help it."

"I know," said Charlie, more warmly this time. "We all know, and we all understand."

And I had tried. Boy had I tried. I'd even put myself into Charlie's hands and let her and Juan load my details onto the internet and fix me up with online dates in the hope of meeting someone else and quashing the feelings I had towards Ted.

But it didn't work...far from it. The whole process of dating men who ranged from stark raving mad to mildly bonkers just confirmed how much I liked Ted and how much I wanted him and no one else.

"If you're in love with him, you need to let him know," said Juan Pedro.

"How on earth do I do that?" I asked. I wasn't going to ring him and declare undying love, was I? Especially since he hadn't shown the remotest sign that he missed me or wanted me back.

"Maybe hire a man with a mandolin to stand outside his window strumming love songs as dancing girls leap and twirl and you recite poetry while being held aloft?"

"I could do," I said. "But he might just take out a restraining order."

A gentle silence fell over the group, and I assumed they were all trying to think of ways in which I could win back Ted without the use of mandolins. But then I saw Dave nudge Charlie and I knew something was wrong. The silence was loud and threatening.

What I didn't know was that my world was about to collapse in on me.

"What's with all the nudging?" I asked. "You have to share any secrets and jokes with me...it's the law."

"It's nothing," said Juan. "We're just thinking about you and Ted and how to get you back together."

But I could tell from Charlie's face that something was amiss. I could see the worry shrouding her as she sat there, staring ahead, not commenting.

"Charlie," I said. "What's wrong? You look really worried."

"I don't know whether to say something," she said, glancing at Juan. "But you're my best friend and I'd rather tell you everything."

"Yes, tell me everything. Always tell me everything."

"We think Ted has been seeing someone."

"What do you mean?"

Charlie shrugged. "He was in the pub with a woman. Ted looked like he was on a date. That's all."

I felt a tightness pull at my chest. It was like I'd been shot. I could almost feel the physical pain of the words: Ted-has-met-someone-else.

"Ted? He can't be with someone else."

"It could have been a casual date," said Charlie. "You know - just a friendly drink."

"So, he didn't have his arm around her, or kiss her, or anything?"

"Well, yes - he did have his arm around her. That's why we think he was on a date."

3

"Perhaps it was his sister?" I offered, hearing how pathetic I sounded as soon as the words left my mouth.

"I don't think it was his sister."

"How do you know? It could easily have been; she's always having one drama or another. Perhaps she was upset and he put his arm around her to comfort her? Yes, that's probably what it was."

"Oh, for goodness sake, stop pussyfooting around," said Juan, sweeping his hand through his astonishing mane of hair. "Ted was seen snogging this woman outside the pub. It wasn't his sister; it was a date. No one's doing you any favours by hiding that from you. Mary - it probably means nothing at all. He could easily be seeing someone else because he's trying to get over you. But it means it's more important than ever that you tell him you still like him. If you do, he'll come jogging straight back. If you don't - he might develop a relationship with this new woman."

I stared at Juan like he had four noses. I couldn't believe what I'd just heard.

"Snogging? He was snogging someone outside the pub?"

"It was probably just a drunken snog that meant nothing at all."

"Who saw them? Are you sure about the snogging bit? I mean, it's very difficult to see properly when it's dark. Whoever it was might have thought they saw them snogging, but didn't. Perhaps she had something in her teeth, and he was trying to remove it?"

"What, with his tongue?" said Juan.

I stared at the ground.

"Who saw them?" I asked.

"Me," said Dave.

Dave was my drop-dead gorgeous neighbour, living in the flat below. He stared at the ground as he spoke, not making eye contact.

"Dave, you drink a lot. You could easily have been mistaken."

"Thanks very much," said Dave.

"No, but you know what I mean…"

"I'd had one pint. He was with another girl. I didn't recognise her or anything."

"What did she look like? Was she fat?"

That was what I really wanted to know the answer to. Was he kissing her instead of me because she was thin?

"I didn't see her clearly. Sorry."

"You must have been able to see whether she was fat."

"Honestly, I walked past them. It was only as I caught sight of his face from the side, that I realised who it was, and then it was too late to go back and peer at her to see whether she was fat."

"No, no, no. That's where you're wrong. It is never too late to go back and peer at someone who is kissing my boyfriend."

"I know you're upset. You just need to ring Ted and tell him how you feel about him."

"What colour hair did she have?"

"Dark, I think," said Dave.

"Ha. Good," I replied. Dave looked relieved to have answered a question properly.

"Call him," said Juan.

"And how the hell am I going to do that?"

Juan mimed picking up a phone, and made phone ringing noises.

"Hi, is that Ted," he said, in a high-pitched voice that was supposed to be an imitation of mine. "It's Mary here. I hope you're OK, and I'm sorry to ring completely out of the blue, but I wanted to ask how you are, and most importantly I wanted to tell you that I miss you. I'd love to meet up for a drink whenever you're free."

"Yeah, cos that's really going to work, isn't it?" I said. "Our relationship collapsed and he's moved on. No doubt the new woman is beautiful, slim and adorable...not like me."

Juan's face had turned red and he looked genuinely cross. "You're the loveliest person in the world... You are gorgeous and fun and fabulous to be around. Any man would die to be with you. Ted hasn't found someone better; he's found someone new because you're not available. I wish women would realise this and stop undervaluing themselves. You need to let him know that you want him back, that you adore him and see a future with him."

I looked at Juan. I wanted to thank him for his kind words, but the tears were spreading at the back of my eyes and threatening to pour forth, and I didn't want to cry again. I'd done too much crying in the weeks since Ted and I had split up. I didn't want my friends feeling sorry for me.

I left the room on the pretence of going to the loo. I needed to get away from the kindly looks and soft words. And I needed to try to escape from the images of Ted kissing another woman. No, not kissing, SNOGGING another woman. That was worse. Snogging implied lust, desire and urgency. Damn.

I closed the bathroom door behind me and gripped the sink, almost pulling the wretched thing off the wall. Tears began to trace their way down my face, leaving a greasy track in my make-up.

Then, a gentle knock on the door. "Open up, Angel, let me in."

It was Charlie. As I knew it would be.

I'll be out in a minute," I said. "I'm fine, just going to the loo."

"No, you're not," she said. "Open the door."

I flushed the chain to continue the pretence, then wiped my eyes to make it look as if I hadn't been crying. But when I saw Charlie, I couldn't pretend any more. I burst into tears and collapsed on her shoulder, gulping huge breaths of air and ugly crying into her favourite silk top.

"You just need to tell him how you feel," she said.

"How? I never see him."

"Call him."

"I can't. There's too much water under the bridge for that. I honestly can't."

"Well, we'll have to arrange for you to bump into him."

"It's not going to work. I never bump into him."

"I bet you could if you wanted to. Let's make a 'bumping into Ted' plan."

"No. I just need to forget about him and move on. He won't want me back. Look at me...I'm so fat. I've done nothing but eat and drink since we split up." I'd replaced kisses from Ted with chocolate bars from the corner shop, and was a swap that had not done a great deal for my appearance.

Charlie smiled and hugged me.

"You look lovely," she said. "You always look lovely."

"Sure, but I bet the girl he was kissing was really skinny, wasn't she?"

"I don't know."

"Of course she was," I said. "I can picture her now - small, with tiny wrists and little hips like an underdeveloped toddler, probably with gorgeous auburn hair down to her minuscule waist...in short - everything I'm not."

"You're being irrational now," said Charlie. "There's no way this girl is anywhere near as gorgeous and lovely as you, and there's no way she's as much fun."

"Perhaps I should walk up and down outside his flat telling jokes?" I said. "I could show him just how much fun I am by cracking Tim Vine-style one-liners in quick succession while walking up and down his garden path."

"Maybe," said Charlie. "Or maybe he'll have you arrested for breach of the peace."

"I love him," I said, solemnly.

"Then call him."

"I can't. That feels so desperate. And why doesn't he call me? Why is it left to me to do the running around?"

"Because he doesn't think you like him. He's probably heard about all the dates you've been going on."

"Oh God, I've really messed up here, haven't I?"

"No, you haven't. Not at all. You two are meant to be together. And...I've just had a thought."

"What?"

"Well, you'll see him on my 30th, won't you? You'll have a whole evening to beguile him."

"Yessss," I said, suddenly feeling much brighter. "I'd forgotten that he was coming."

Charlie, Juan and I had been organising Charlie's birthday party for months. Juan and I had been to check out a tonne of swanky venues...hotels, central London bars, restaurants and private rooms. But then, one night, Charlie told us that what she would really like was a small party at home, so that's where it was happening.

"I invited Ted when we were all in the pub a while ago, and

he said he'd come. To be honest, I was going to withdraw the invitation after you split up."

"Don't withdraw it. Send him a reminder," I said, suddenly brightening up as I felt the clouds lift to reveal a beautiful blue sky before me. "Your party is in a month and a half: I'll spend the next six weeks getting myself as fit and gorgeous as possible so that when I see him, I look amazing."

"Or you could call him?"

"No, I've got this. I need a six-week plan to transform myself, then when I walk into your party he'll fall at my feet and demand that I go back to him."

"OK," said Charlie, looking a little dubious. "But you know you don't have to change in any way, don't you? You're lovely as you are."

"Sure," I replied, but my mind had already cast itself out into the future, onto a sunny day six weeks hence, and I was drifting into Charlie's party, watching as everyone spun round and stared at me, open-mouthed. Then there would be Ted...standing there, probably leaning casually against a sideboard or something with a smile on his lovely face. "Come here, Mary," he'd say. "I've missed you so much."

CHAPTER TWO

t was the first day of the six-week plan and, to my shame, it had all gone pear-shaped by 8am. I'd completely forgotten. I was so moody after not sleeping all night for thinking about Ted that before I realised what I was doing, I had put two pieces of bread into the toaster, then another two, laid them on a plate, covered in butter, with a big lump of cheese and a packet of crisps, and gobbled the whole lot up. It was the most ridiculous of breakfasts, by anyone's standards, but it was particularly ridiculous given my commitment to losing a ton of weight in six weeks.

I reached for an apple and a banana afterwards, hoping in vain that some of the goodness in the fresh fruit would somehow erase the calorie-laden cheesiness of the initial food intake. I don't think it did. The only thing it did was to pile on a few more calories. And the thought of that was so depressing that I grabbed another packet of crisps before sitting down on the sofa next to Juan.

"I've eaten more calories than I'm supposed to eat in the whole day and it's not 9am yet," I announced.

"What are you after? Some sort of prize?"

"I'd like some self-control please," I said, popping a big cheese and onion crisp into my mouth.

Dieting was hard. Food was so nice: it helped you forget your problems and feel all warm and comforted.

"Juan, I'm not very good at diets," I said, tipping the rest of the crisps into my mouth as my lovely Spanish friend smiled at me.

"They are terrible things," he agreed. "You should just come to Pilates with me...you will start to feel better about yourself by the end of the first session, work muscles you didn't even know you had, and hold yourself more elegantly. Did I tell you I am going to train as a Pilates instructor?"

"Are you? Christ, I'm hopeless at anything like that. I went on a yoga weekend once and almost killed myself. Did I tell you about that? Some bloke came down from Downward Dog and his tackle fell out of his shorts and thumped onto the ground like a pound of Cumberland sausages. Very distressing."

"You told me," replied Juan. "Many times."

"Is that why you want to train as a Pilates instructor? So, you can see lots of Cumberland sausages falling out of shorts?"

"No, lovely. That's not why," he said, smiling and kissing me on the top of my head. "You are nuts, you know."

"Yep, so people keep telling me. But I want to be slim and beautiful, not nuts."

"You are beautiful," he said quickly.

"Aha, but not slim. You missed out slim."

"You have a gorgeous womanly body...you are very attractive," he said.

"If you weren't gay, would you fancy me?"

"Totally," he said. "No question. I fancy you even though I am gay."

"Good," I replied, then we sat there in silence for a while, just looking at one another.

"I need a head start in all this weight loss," I said. "Something to give me a boost. What do you think I should do? Maybe go to the doctors and see whether I can get some pills?"

"No, Mary. You mustn't do that. Just come to Pilates with me and I'll help you to develop respect for your body."

"No - I don't want to do any of that new age nonsense. Respect? No thanks. I want drugs."

"Such a bad idea. You'll get addicted to them and find yourself in all sorts of trouble."

"But at least I'd be thin and in trouble. Oh, I know what I need - do you remember that weight loss camp I went on? I need something like that; to motivate me and get me on the right track."

"But you hated it."

"I know, but the stakes are high now. If I lose weight, Ted will come running back to me and we'll be together forever. If I don't - I'm destined to be all alone for the rest of my life."

"I don't think it's quite that bad."

"It feels like it."

Charlie joined us in the sitting room. She'd practically set up home here since Juan moved in with me. She was eating a piece of toast covered in jam and held a large mug of hot chocolate in her hands. I felt a wave of longing wash over me, even as we discussed the weight loss camp, I really wanted jam on toast.

"You won't believe this," said Juan. "Mary wants to go back on a weight loss camp again."

"I don't *want* to," I said. "But I have to. I need to get cracking on this diet, and I feel like I need a kick start. It's either that or drugs..."

"Well drugs would be an unwise move. I'd go for the weight loss camp over drugs any day. Have you spoken to Dawn? She's always being offered free trips, isn't she? Perhaps she could help you out."

"Ooooo...I could do," I said. "That's not a bad shout at all."

Dawn was a very overweight old school friend (fatter than me - yay!) who ran a blog called 'Two Fat Ladies' about her life as an overweight woman. She did most of the activities for the blog with her large friend which is why it was called 'Two Fat Ladies' but I'd been on a few holidays for her when her friend wasn't available, and reported back on them - sending in updates, embarrassing photos and excruciating videos. The weight loss camp had come through Dawn.

"I'll text her," I said. It felt a bit too early to call her, so I just sent a simple message: "Give me a call when you get a spare minute."

My phone rang within seconds, and Dawn's name flashed up. Blimey, that was quick.

"What's the matter?" she asked. She sounded panicky and worried, as if we'd committed a crime together and I was ringing her to tell her that the police were on to us.

"Nothing's the matter," I said. "Well, apart from the simple fact that my boyfriend is seeing someone new."

"Oh," she replied.

"Look - do you still review holidays on your Fat Lady blog?"

"Yes. Why? Is there a problem?"

"No, no problem."

Why did she think there was a problem? This was turning out to be the weirdest conversation ever.

"I was just being really cheeky, actually. I wondered whether there were any holidays that you wanted covering, preferably with a health and fitness theme, you know - for the Fat Lady blog."

"Oh, I see, I see. Oh, OK. No problem, that's fine," said Dawn, sounding oddly relieved.

There was a pause.

"Actually, there was a trip on offer. I turned it down, but I could see whether it's still available. How soon could you go?"

"Anytime," I said. "They owe me time off at work. I'd like to get out of this place so I don't bump into Ted and his new girl-friend. I can go any time."

"Well, it was a health and fitness trip to Italy but the flight's tomorrow morning. I've got stuff going on here so can't go, but I could see whether it's still available."

"Oh, could you? That would be wonderful."

"I'll get back to you when I know for sure," she said. "And you're absolutely sure you're OK? I mean - we're OK, aren't we?"

"Yes, of course we are. Why wouldn't we be?"

"No reason, just checking. Leave it with me and I'll chase that Italy trip and come back to you later. OK?"

"That's great. Thanks so much."

I put the phone down and turned to Juan. "That was strange, she was acting really oddly, as if she was waiting for some terrible news from me or something."

"She was probably half asleep," he said. "It's not yet 9am on a Saturday morning, most civilised people are still in their beds."

"Yeah, I guess."

Ten minutes later I had a text from Dawn.

"All on for tomorrow. Flight is at 7am. Hotel is called Masseria Bianca. All the details including link to tickets coming in an email. If you need anything else, let me know. Sorry about everything, Dawn."

I READ IT TO JUAN.

"Well, that's good news," he said. "You've got yourself another free bloody holiday. I have no idea how you do it."

"Yeah, but what does 'sorry about everything' mean? And why's she being so friendly? You know Dawn - she's never friendly."

"Perhaps she's sorry she hasn't been in touch before, or invited you to any trips recently? Perhaps she's really sorry about you and Ted splitting up?"

"Yeah, perhaps," I said.

"A flight at 7am is going to be fun after the wedding reception tonight. We'll have to make sure we don't stay too late."

"What wedding reception?"

"Oh, for heaven's sake, Mary. Pete and Andy are getting married. You promised you'd come with me. We'll just go for a couple of hours; you can be back in bed by 10pm."

"OK," I said. "But we have to be back early. I'll pack everything and sort out all the tickets tonight, then I'll be ready to leave at the crack of dawn."

"The crack of Dawn!" said Juan with an enormous guffaw. "Up at the crack of Dawn! No wonder she was a bit funny with you on the phone."

Later that evening...

By 11pm I was slouched on a burgundy banquette that looked as if it had been lifted from a 1980s British Rail train, chatting away to a stranger. I had forgotten all about my early morning spa trip as I told the very drunk woman my woes.

"You see, I love him," I slurred.

Drunk woman didn't respond. She might have been asleep. I didn't know, and it didn't matter...I was talking anyway.

"And he loves me. We're meant to be together."

"Come on, Mary. I really think we should go," said Juan, joining us. "You have to leave early in the morning."

I noticed that a man had also joined the woman I was talking to.

"What about my new friend here? I'm telling her about Ted."

"Mary, my love, that's not a woman, that's you in the mirror. Now - come on, let's go home."

CHAPTER THREE

$\mathcal{T}$he sound of the alarm clock thundered through me. My head pounded and my hands shook.

Good God alive.

It was as if the devil himself had come up from the fiery pits of hell to bite my throat. In front of me I could just about make out Juan, at the end of the bed - a fuzzy, pale image, like the Ghost of Christmas Past.

"For the love of all that is holy, what's going on," I squealed. "Why are we getting up in the middle of the night?"

"It's not the middle of the night, it's early in the morning. You're going to Italy, remember. You have to leave in 10 minutes."

Juan put the light on, sending a blast of hideous brightness into the room.

"I am so not going to Italy," I said, pulling the duvet over my pounding head. I felt like I might be sick at any moment.

I also felt uncomfortable. Why was I uncomfortable?

"You have to get up now. NOW." Juan sounded very insistent, but there was no way on earth that I could get out of bed and negotiate my way to Italy. It couldn't happen.

"NOW."

Juan tore the duvet off me, and gave a look at horror as he looked down at me.

"Sweet Jesus, did you not even get undressed," he said. "How drunk were you?"

"I don't remember anything after the tray races," I said, easing myself out of bed, holding my head. Juan was disgusted by my failure to undress last night but I was secretly thrilled. It would save me 10 minutes of faffing around trying to work out which jeans I looked less fat in and what top covered me up most comprehensively.

"What tray races?"

"Don't you remember? I introduced a game of winter Olympics and went sliding across the floor on trays and did slalom skiing with plastic plates strapped to our feet. The groom was really good at the curling event if I remember correctly - he was masterful with the broom. It's all a bit vague but I think I broke a tray. Not sure."

I walked into the bathroom, brushed my teeth and splashed cold water on my still made-up face.

"I should have withdrawn from the tournament after the heats," I said, as I surveyed the bags under my eyes, and the bruises on my elbows. "I'm not a natural winter Olympian."

"Come on, you nutter, quickly, the cab will be here in 5 minutes. Go and get dressed."

"I am dressed," I pointed out. "I just need to pack."

"PACK? Have you not packed?"

"Relax, it's fine. I'll do it now. I'll meet you in the sitting room."

Juan jabbered away to himself in Spanish as he wandered into the front room while I threw trainers and gym kit into a bag. I had a sudden flash back to being sick in the loos the night before. I think that was after I'd judged the ice dance event. Christ alive.

"Taxi," said Juan, swinging open the door, and gently pushing me out. "Have a brilliant time. Text me when you get there so I know you've arrived safely and haven't died of alcohol poisoning en route."

"Will do," I said, easing myself gently into the back of the car, and promptly falling asleep. We arrived at Heathrow airport and despite a headache that was now banging inside my skull, I somehow found my way to the right place to drop my bag off before queueing for security. One of the only (the only) joys of an early morning flight was that they didn't seem to be too many people around. I went through the whole process with uncommon speed, and had soon plonked myself in a restaurant to order breakfast.

I was about to go on a three-day spa, so it couldn't possibly hurt if I had a nice breakfast before going, could it? I'd have worked it off by lunchtime, in any case. But when I looked at the menu, I felt so tired I couldn't even work out what I wanted to eat., I was also a little concerned that if I ate anything, I'd be immediately sick. I ordered a cup of tea and texted Juan to let him know that I'd made it to the airport safely.

Two cups later and some strong painkillers, and I was ready to get on the plane. I don't remember much about this...I remember the plane being called, and I recall clambering onto

it and having the usual indignity of asking for a seatbelt exten-
der, but then I think I must have fallen asleep.

"Ladies and gentlemen, welcome to Bari Airport. For your
safety and comfort, please remain seated with your seat belt
fastened until the Captain turns off the Fasten Seat Belt sign."

Blimey. I'd missed the whole flight...including breakfast.
Hoorah! My Mediterranean diet retreat was getting off to a
most tremendous start. Perhaps that's all I had to do to lose
weight: get so utterly blind drunk that I couldn't eat anything.

We clambered off the plane and made our way through the
packed arrivals hall. I collected my luggage and looked along
the row of drivers holding signs featuring a range of Italian
sounding names. At the end of the line there was a rather
dapper, older Italian man clutching a sign with the words 'Mr
and Mrs Brown' on it.

"That's me!" I said. "Well - I'm Mary Brown. Or perhaps
you're waiting for someone else?"

"I am waiting for couple," he said. "Newly married couple.
Where is your husband?"

"I don't have a husband."

"I thought you were coming here from your wedding. There
has not been a wedding?" he said.

"There is no husband, no wedding," I said. "Just me." Christ, I
needed this like a hole in the head.

He looked at me for a while, slightly dubious, as if he
thought I may be concealing a husband.

"Shall we go?" I said. No man was going to emerge from the
plane and announce himself as my husband, so it seemed point-
less to stand there.

"Okay," he said, taking my bag from me and leading the way

through the carpark as he talked on his phone, jabbering away in Italian.

"Prego, Prego..." he said, opening the car door for me:

"Hotel is expecting you and husband."

"I understand that. But I have no husband."

He tutted and I found myself apologising before sinking back into the seat and looking out of the window as we eased into the traffic. The talk of husbands was not what I needed, and as we drove away from the airport, into the countryside, I fought to hold back the tears filling my eyes behind the sunglasses I'd nicked from Juan. I watched as the beautiful scenery passed by. It was still raining but it didn't spoil the beauty... The magnificence of the rows of olive trees as far as the eye could see. Flowers along the roadside that seemed to grow up magically through the rocks. I just wished Ted were here with me.

As the rain got heavier, I watched the men working in the olive groves in short-sleeved shirts; they rushed around, inadequately shielding their hair from the weather with their hands.

"They silly people. Get wet. Very bad."

"Yes," I replied.

"You no husband," he said.

"Nope, no husband."

"Very bad," he said. "Very bad."

"Yep," I said.

CHAPTER FOUR

*A*fter driving for almost an hour, we turned into a driveway leading to the beautiful Masseria where I would be staying for the next few days. It looked stunning - the place was a magnificent chalk white colour - like a solitary snowdrop popping up on a lawn, as it sat in the green hills and olive groves of southern Italy.

There was a beautiful pool outside and a multitude of olive trees potted and dotted around. The entrance to the Masseria was surrounded by beautiful red flowers in terracotta pots. Even in my post-drinking, Ted-missing misery, the vibrant beauty of the flowers against the limestone walls reflected in the pool sitting silently before it, hit me with all its might. It was hard to imagine anywhere more beautiful or relaxing in which to spend time. My mood, which had been considerably dented by the driver's insistence that I should have a husband with me, and my decision to half-kill myself by drinking gallons of vodka while playing winter Olympics the night before, lifted joyously at the sight of the place where I would be staying.

Inside the reception area I was welcomed warmly by a dark-skinned beauty, with lips the same vibrant red as the flowers outside. "My name Lola," she said, offering an elegant hand with perfect nails. She had one of those amazing figures that Italian women in films have... You know, very curvy and sexy but also slender. Her wavy black hair rippled down over her slender shoulders.

"Welcome to Masseria Bianca," she added. "Your husband is here?"

Oh God, here we go again.

"I don't know why people keep asking about my husband. It's just me here," I said. I was about to launch into the fact that I wasn't married and didn't even have a boyfriend and that he was seeing someone else and quite frankly it was an appalling state of affairs because I was very much in love with Ted, and hope to winning back and thought that might be easier if I lost weight and looked a bit better... But - remarkably for me - I kept my mouth shut.

"I am very sorry for confusion. Please follow me," she said with a toss of hair that was so shiny it looked like liquid, and I followed her gorgeous curvy figure as she wriggled down the corridor, click-clacking on her lovely little kitten heels. While she swayed along, I clumped behind her in yesterday's clothes. I looked down to see beer stains on my white trainers and on the tops of my jeans from when I tried to do winter Olympics with a pint in my hand. I really needed to be more elegant and lady-like if I was going to win Ted back. More like Lola.

I looked at her again as she glided along the carpet with her gently swaying motion, like she was moving to an imaginary drum beat. She reminded me of one of the gorgeous women that Downstairs Dave always has at his beck and call. I almost wanted to take a video of her swaying hips and send it to him to show him what he was missing. But I figured that was too weird...even for me. First, I had turned up without a husband, when I was expected to provide one, then I was taking videos of the bottoms of the attractive female members of staff. Nope. That would not be on.

Lola unlocked the bedroom door, handed me the key, then pushed it open and stood back for me to walk inside. The room was incredible...a four-poster bed took pride of place, with sweeping voile curtains in the lightest gossamer. There were rose petals everywhere, balloons, a huge bottle of champagne and a large basket of chocolates on the table. The only thing ruining it was a big silk banner offering congratulations on my recent wedding.

I stood there and looked at it, then turned to Lola.

"I'm not married, I've never been married, I don't even have a boyfriend. I don't know why you're doing this. Why does everyone think I'm married? My boyfriend and I have split up and he's met someone else - someone skinny and beautiful like you, and I came here to escape from it all and lose weight, and now you're all asking me about being married. I don't know why you..."

"I'm so sorry," she said, interrupting my flow. "I don't know what has happened. It is written down that you were come as a couple to honeymoon room." She tapped away on her phone, and in minutes a small army of cleaners had arrived...they swept up the rose petals, pulled down the sign and removed the balloons. In no time at all the room looked like a normal, but very sumptuous, hotel room.

"Again, I'm so sorry," she said. Behind her a tall gangly man appeared.

"My name is Massimo. I am deputy manager. I'm so sorry. It is terrible mistake," he said. "The couple that is coming today is no longer coming, the wedding called off. Is the best room in the hotel so we give to you. I'm afraid message did not get through that the couple not coming, so they have decorate room for wedding and on your honeymoon. I'm very sorry."

"It's fine," I said to the rather dapper looking Italian with his embarrassed smile, his young eyes and his floppy dark hair that kept falling slightly into his eyes. I had to stop myself from pushing it gently aside so he could see properly.

"It's no problem at all," I said again.

Behind me the cleaners came back in and picked up the champagne and the chocolates and starting messing with the contents of the mini bar before they went to leave the room.

"Don't take those," I said.

"But no madam, you are on the Mediterranean diet retreat, we must ask you not to drink or have chocolate."

"What? Surely a Mediterranean diet will be full of champagne?"

"You will be allowed a glass of red wine made here on the premises that is full of antioxidants if you request, but only one glass and only in evening."

I opened my mouth to object before remembering that I was alone in the honeymoon suite while the man I loved was dancing around Surrey with his slim girlfriend. I needed to get myself looking good as quickly as possible.

"Of course," I said.

They walked out with the champagne and the basket full of chocolates and - I admit, dear readers - my heart sank a little. I knew it would be worth it in the end, but then - in that moment - I wanted to bury my fat face into the basket of chocolate and eat all the way through to the straw beneath them.

"Lunch will be in Ristorante Soleggiato in one hour's time," said Massimo. "It will be with Flavia, the manager of this hotel."

"Oh, how lovely, thank you." I said.

"Can I just double-check with you: your husband? Is not coming. No?"

"No," I said calmly. "There is no husband."

"Very many sorrys," he said, backing out of the door while bowing respectfully. "And Dawn. She is on her way?"

"Is she?"

"Yes. She is now at airport and will be getting on plane in one hour."

"Oh. I don't know. I didn't realise she was coming. I'll call her now."

"Very good," said Massimo. "Very good."

Once he had gone, I called Dawn. I really hoped she wasn't on her way out here. She's quite a difficult character, is Dawn. I know that sounds a bit cruel, given that she fixed up this break for me, but I do find her quite challenging company.

"Dawn," I said. "It's me, Mary, I'm at the hotel in Italy."

"Oh good. Is there a problem?" she said.

"No - it's lovely. I was just calling because they said you were coming out here."

"To Italy?"

"Yes, the Assistant Manager said you were on your way."

"Why would I be on my way?"

"I don't know. That's what I was calling to find out."

"No, I'm not on my way. You're at Massaria Bianca, yes?"

"Yes."

"Why would I be coming out?"

"I don't know. They thought you were so I thought I'd better phone up and check."

"You're checking on me?" said Dawn.

"No, just checking to see whether you're planning to come out."

"You've heard, haven't you?" said Dawn. "All this suddenly ringing me out of the blue to see whether I can offer you a holiday, then ringing me from the hotel for no good reason. Just ask me what you want to ask me, Mary?"

"Dawn, I genuinely have no idea what on earth you are talking about."

"OK. I'll make it easier for you. Yes - it is me who is going out with Ted."

"You're…. you're what? Ted? Ted who? Not my Ted?"

"No, not your Ted, Mary. He's not your Ted. The two of you split up months ago. I've been seeing him; I thought that's why you were ringing me...to ask about him?"

"No. I, I didn't know. I was genuinely just ringing because they asked me whether you were coming out."

"Well, I don't know why they thought that. Look - I'm sorry - I know it's shit. I genuinely don't want to hurt you or anything. We just sort of clicked."

"How long have you been seeing him?"

"Just a few weeks."

I couldn't really talk after that. I just lay back on the bed with the phone by my side. I could hear Dawn saying 'hello, hello?' and apologising if she'd hurt me, then she hung up, and I carried on lying there, looking at the ceiling and trying to banish thoughts of Ted and Dawn from my mind.

CHAPTER FIVE

"*H*e's going out with BFD?" said Juan for about the fourth time while I sobbed uncontrollably down the phone.

"Yep."

"Are you sure?" said Juan.

"That's what she said."

"But what on earth does he see in Big Fat Dawn?"

"I don't know. I don't want to stay here anymore; I want to come home."

I was sobbing like my heart was about to break in two.

"Hey, come on angel. Stop crying. Ted probably just wanted company and she was around. I'm sure he's not going out with her."

"Dawn's not even good company," I wailed. "Not in anyone's book. And I know I shouldn't criticise but she's about 25 stone. And she's got a really nasty streak. Ted's such a soft, loving man...they are not right at all."

"No. They are not. You should be with Ted. We all know that."

"What if they're in love," I said through great, big sobs.

Juan replied but I couldn't hear him over the sound of my own wailing.

"I doubt they have been together long," he repeated, raising his voice so I could hear him. "The impression I get is that they've only been on a couple of dates."

"She said weeks. They have been seeing one another for weeks. She was worried that I was calling to confront her about her relationship with Ted. Which means she knows what she's done is wrong. She's gone smashing straight through the girl code. I bet they end up getting married, and I'll be standing in the road outside sobbing as she sweeps past me in a massive meringue of a dress."

"I think you might be overthinking this. There's no suggestion that they are dating, let alone getting married."

I didn't reply. I knew I was being dramatic and ridiculous, but it hurt so much I couldn't help myself.

"I'm coming out there," said Juan, suddenly. "I'll get a flight sorted and I will be there in the morning."

"Really?"

"Yep. You sound so sad. I'll come out and join you. Email me all the information about which airport I have to go to and where the hotel is. I'll call you later when I've fixed up a flight, OK?"

"Will you really do that?"

"I will," said Juan. "I'll be there around midday. Keep smiling, angel. This is all going to be OK."

"Text me when you're on the way from the airport and I'll

make sure I'm here in the room. We might have to sneak you in, though."

"Sneaking is fine," he said. "I'm a big fan of sneaking."

I sent Juan a plethora of emails about the hotel, where it was, what was the easiest way to get here, then I lay back on the bed and looked up at the intricately carved ceiling once more. It would be lovely to have Juan here. I didn't want to be alone after finding out about Dawn.

I looked over at the minibar in the corner. It was smiling at me, flirting with me, urging me towards it. "Come on, Mary. You know you'll feel better after a small tube of pringles," it was saying.

I did this too much...allowed the voice in my head to take over at the slightest chance.

I fought to introduce another voice - one which reminded me that being slimmer, healthier and fitter was a great thing, regardless of whether I ended up back with Ted. I'd feel better if I could get fitter and stronger...more wonderful than any amount of chocolate would make me feel. 'Hey - imagine running into Ted and Dawn when you're lovely and slim?' said the new voice.

'Ah, but imagine how delicious a gin and tonic would taste?' said the original voice.

I lay on the bed with these competing voices playing tennis across my brain, then I sat up, stepped out of bed, opened the minibar, and took a peek inside.

I needn't have bothered. The voices in my head had been wasting their time. In the minibar there were six bottles of water, and a tiny dish with about three olives in it. A note next to it said that all food would be provided for me over the week because I was on the 'Mediterranean retreat' but that if I found myself getting very hungry, I could nibble on an olive.

How the hell would an olive ever be enough to satisfy a hunger pang? In whose world would that be sufficient to keep hunger at bay?

No one's.

The phone on the bedside cabinet rang with a loud, old-fashioned ring. "Madam, I hope you are settling in well," said a female voice, presumably the lovely Lola. "Just to remind you that the manager will meet you for lunch in 30 minutes."

It was the very last thing that I wanted to do. I wanted to order chips and pudding on room service and stay here, eating it until Juan arrived. I lay back on the bed, and felt my face crease up again as more tears came. I knew that every little thing would make me cry now...thoughts of Ted, seeing couples together, even an invitation to lunch with the manager.

I felt particularly hurt that it was Dawn who Ted was seeing, not just because she was supposed to be a friend, of sorts; but because she wasn't glamorous by any stretch of the word, and was really fat. That meant he must really like her. It wasn't a distracting fling with a glamour puss, but the real thing.

Damn her.

Damn him.

Damn me for not calling him and telling him how I felt.

LUNCH WAS HELD IN THE MAIN RESTAURANT – A BEAUTIFUL, characterful room with beams and an enchanting open fire. It wasn't what I was expecting at all. Outside, the Masseria was sleek and elegant. Inside it had a very fussy old-world charm. There were straw baskets full of wood dotted around the room, as well as old fashioned rugs like the ones they have in Hampton Court Palace. Big vases were filled with a mixture of dried and fresh flowers. And, of course, there were the obligatory olive trees in terracotta pots.

The manageress was called Flavia. She met me at the doors to the restaurant and guided me to our table.

Waiters buzzed around us, as soon as we sat down, offering the most delicious-looking bread, wine and olives. I said yes to everything. It all looked so lovely.

"No thank you," said the manageress in perfect English.

Shit, I should have said 'no'. I just automatically say yes to food. How do people say 'no'? It's so hard to say 'no'. We're all programmed to eat whenever food is offered, surely.

"I'm not going to have bread because I'm on a diet," said Flavia, brushing away the basket being proffered.

"A diet?" I asked, astounded. The woman didn't have an ounce of fat on her. If she thought she needed to lose weight, goodness knows what she thought of me.

"You don't need to lose any weight at all. You look lovely," I said.

"You are very kind, but I have a little fat to lose on my waistline."

Having a little fat to lose on my waistline would be the stuff of dreams. I didn't even have a waistline, and hadn't for 10 years. All that I felt when I touched my middle was blubber. But I decided not to share this with her.

I was presented with a Mediterranean menu to reflect the fact that I was here on a health trip, rather than to indulge. I peeked at it with trepidation. If the mini bar treats consisted of olives, then heaven knows what the diet menu had in store for me... air dried grass and a small bag of sky? A grain of salt and a drop of water?

The relief on my face when I saw there were about six courses must have been obvious to my host.

She reached over and touched my hand gently. "We don't starve our guests!" she said,

I looked down at her hand on mine. That small moment of affection, the feel of her warm touch, brought tears to my eyes. I really loved Ted. I didn't know what to do. How would I cope if I never won him back?

"The Mediterranean diet is full of healthy natural locally produced ingredients," Flavia said, unaware of the dark alleyways into which I was wandering in my mind. "There is no sugar or milk, very little starch and lots of healthy protein. Mainly it's full of vegetables but don't worry if that sounds boring, you will find they are delicious when combined with our home-made olive oil and with lemon from the trees that are growing outside your room."

"That does sound lovely," I said, forcing myself to smile.

I decided to order the fennel salad, on her advice, and she suggested following it with the lentil soup and prawns with almonds. This did not sound like a proper grown-up sized meal to me - where were the chips? Chips were vegetables.

"Do you do many health retreats?" she asked.

I'd have thought that by looking at the size of me, she could have worked out for herself.

I explained that I'd only done one...a kind of military fitness camp that almost killed me. I lost weight on it though. But I put it all back on again and much more.

"Here we go," said Flavia, as a team of waiters approached brandishing plates with those silver domes on top. I think they are called cloches. They placed the plates down and lifted the domes in unison.

The tiniest amount of food sat on my plate.

"Bon Appetit," said Flavia, tasting the smallest morsel and swooning in delight. I filled my fork with considerably more of the fennel and shoved it into my mouth.

"Oh my God," I mumbled with my mouth full. "This is bloody lovely." The fennel salad was beyond delicious, with its lemony flavour making it both sweet and sharp at the same time. It also had garlic in it and slivers of spring onion...all the things I'd normally steer clear of when ordering food in a restaurant but all the flavours together were wonderful. I quickly finished the lot and looked up to see Flavia had pushed her plate away after just a taste.

"Don't you like it?"

"I adore it, but I have to lose weight. If I have one little taste of everything instead of eating it all, I feel satisfied. All the different flavours and fresh food will make you feel full up even though you aren't eating as much."

"I should do that, but I have no self-control. None at all."

She smiled. "You will lose weight this week, don't worry. I have to lose weight urgently because I am getting married soon. I need to fit into my dress."

"Oh, how lovely. When do you get married?"

"In three weeks. To the fitness manager here. You will meet him later."

"Congratulations."

After the fennel came another salad to refresh our palates. I nibbled at a little of it, instead of wolfing it down like I normally do, then pushed the plate aside, smiling at Flavia.

I felt very confident and in control of life when I left food on the plate. We had the soup next, and I did the same...I had a taste, ate a prawn, and pushed the rest aside. This was a whole new me.

"So, you have your first fitness class this evening, at 6pm, then you are welcome to come to the dining room for dinner after that. Or you may have room service. It's completely up to you. You decide."

"Sure," I said, standing up. "Thank you very much for lunch."

We shook hands and I walked away, hoping that the 'new me' was as good at coping with the demands of fitness as she was at denying herself food.

It turned out that the fitness session was aquarobics, which was a relief. It's the least stressful of the fitness workouts. I'd take jumping around in waist-deep water over rowing and treadmilling any day of the week.

The instructor's name was Marco, and I could see straight away that he wasn't Flavia's fiancé because this guy was about as gay as it's possible for any man to be.

"OK, just tread water, get your legs moving," he said, marching up and down on the side of the pool in his bright green speedos and white t-shirt. He had very hairy legs and arms and tonnes of jewellery...big gold bracelets and even an ankle bracelet with what looked like shells on it.

Kylie Minogue burst out from the poolside stereo while I lifted my knees higher and waved my arms more frantically. Next, we were onto Madonna. Marco vogued on the side while I did leg kicks and little jumps and clapped along to the beat. It was quite exhausting...or maybe I was quite unfit. And it was a little embarrassing to be leaping around in the pool on my own, but I stuck at it, as the music moved through a playlist from the

1980s. They were clearly used to having older people staying at the hotel.

Whitney Houston burst through the stereo, telling us that she wants to dance with somebody who loves her.

We kept on jogging and swinging our arms through the water, but I could see that Marco was distracted by something. He kept glancing over at the door.

"Ding, dong," he said. "Things are definitely improving around here."

I looked over, following his gaze, just as a man with a purple hat and sparkly jacket, ducked out of sight.

I'd seen that hat before, and there was only one man I knew who wore sparkly clothes. But Juan wasn't due until tomorrow. And the whole plan was for him to sneak into the hotel in an understated fashion, not appear half-way through my fitness classes dripping in sequins. He looked like he was about to star in a cabaret. Perhaps it wasn't Juan, just a friend of Marco's.

We continued our class and I jumped, leaped and pranced through the water, like a salmon in the streams and waterfalls. Well, maybe not like an actual salmon...a bit more like an overweight whale, to be fair. But I continued all the same, and that was the main thing.

CHAPTER SIX

*a*fter thanking Marco, and clambering out of the pool, I rushed down the corridor to my room, wrapped in a soft, white, spa towelling robe (which, by the way is definitely coming home with me). As I rushed along, sopping wet, I wished I'd brought clothes to change into. I really didn't want to bump into an elegant hotel guest while dressed like this. You know what those Italians are like with their immaculate outfits. I really wasn't in the mood to be judged. Then I spotted him, hiding very ineffectively behind a pillar.

"I can see you, Juan," I said. "You're not invisible; you stand out a bloody mile. You're rubbish at going undercover. Make sure you never join MI5, OK?"

"I'm good at hiding," he insisted. "Didn't you see me duck down quickly behind the door while you were doing your jumping in the water thing? Quick as a flash. Boom. Down I went, out of sight."

"Yes, but not a quick enough flash because we both saw you."

"Ah, but you didn't know it was me."

"I kind of guessed that it was. The sequins and a large purple hat are not the best things to wear when you're trying to avoid being seen..."

"Did old gorgeous chops who was running the class see me too?"

"Yes. I think so. It was him glancing over that made me look. He actually said 'ding dong' so I think he quite fancied you. What are you doing here, anyway? I thought you were coming tomorrow. Give me a hug."

"You sounded so sad on the phone. I just wanted to be here with you. I had to check you were OK. Charlie drove me to the airport and I jumped on the first EasyJet flight to Bari. She sends you all the love in the world. How are you feeling?"

"I'm not great," I admitted. "I have this permanent ache inside me and every time I think about the two of them together it's like I've been shot. Oh God. I really want him back, Juan. It hurts."

"I know," said Juan, wrapping his arms around me. "I know how much it hurts. I've been there too. But this doesn't mean you two are over. It just means that it's important to tell him how you feel."

I stood there, looking down, as I dripped all over the carpet. Not speaking.

"Mary, the main thing for you to know is that you're not on your own. You've got Charlie and me and we can help. We'll be there for you; always. Everything's going to be OK."

It didn't feel for one minute as if everything would be OK, but it felt good to have a friend by my side.

"I feel so much better for seeing you," I said, hugging him again.

I really meant it. The next few days would be much more fun with Juan to share them.

We walked back to my room, I let us in and we sat down on the bed. "If you're hungry there are some treats in the mini bar," I said. "Help yourself."

Juan rubbed his hands together, and practically skipped over there.

"Lovely. I'm so hungry. I feel like indulging."

He opened the mini fridge.

"Where? Only teeny olives in here."

"Read the note," I instructed.

Juan read it to himself, moving his lips as he did. I'd noticed him do that before...like a four-year-old who was learning to read. It really endeared him to me.

"This is here in case you get hungry?" he said. "That's crazy. How would that abate anyone's hunger? There has to be more food in here."

Juan searched through to the back of the mini bar to double-check whether he'd missed anything while I lay back on the bed. I needed to have a shower but I couldn't be bothered to move.

"Nothing," said Juan. "Not one thing worth eating."

As he shook his head, as if blaming me for the lack of food, there was a gentle knock on the door.

"It'll just be house-keeping but you better hide," I said. "I don't want them to know you're here with me, they might contact Dawn to complain and I don't want her ringing me to tell me off. I don't want anything to do with that damn woman."

Juan dashed into the garden and ducked behind a potted olive tree. Once again, it was a terrible hiding place.

I opened the hotel door to see Marco standing there.

"You left these," he said, holding out my goggles.

"Oh, thank you for bringing them, and thanks for the class earlier. I really enjoyed it." I took the goggles from him and went to close the door, but he stopped me.

"Oh - the man. He is with you?" Marco was pointing at the bed, I looked around to see Juan's large hat lying on it.

"No. That's my hat," I said, putting it onto my head. "There is no man here."

"Yes, man. Hiding," he said, pointing at the garden. "Very nice man."

I followed Marco's glance into the garden where Juan was very easy to spot...his sequin jacket sparkling away under the garden lights.

"Thank you again for the goggles. I'm so forgetful," I said. "See you soon for more classes."

"Very nice man," repeated Marco, as I closed the door.

I turned to the garden. "Marco saw you," I shouted to him. "Also, he fancies you."

"Oooo, jolly good. Why are you wearing my hat?"

"Long story," I said, taking it off and dropping it onto the bed. "I'm going for a nice hot shower."

"And what are you doing with my sunglasses," he shouted at my retreating back. "I wondered where these had gone."

We went to bed that night after ordering room service and talking at length about my heart break at Ted and Dawn getting together. I knew I was on the verge of boring Juan to death, but I was doing that thing we all do where you are compelled to talk about an issue endlessly as you try to make sense of it, and work out how you could have done things differently.

Juan had nibbled away at the food while I talked: the poor

man had been starving. Strangely, I just didn't feel that hungry. I felt exhausted, though, all the travelling with a hangover and the aquarobics had half killed me. I talked and cried until I had run out of feelings to express. My head hit the pillow and I fell into the deepest sleep.

We hadn't set an alarm clock, of course. It hadn't occurred to either of us that it would be wise to get up before lunch, so the first sounds of the day came with the ringing of the bedside phone, with a message from reception.

"Just to remind you to be at reception for the nutrition course," said a soft, Italian voice.

"OK. What time is the talk?" I said, trying to hide the sleepiness in my voice. Juan was squinting up at me from deep inside the duvet.

"12pm," said the receptionist. I glanced at the clock. It was almost 10 to 12.

"Of course," I said.

"It's in the kitchens which are situated just past the reception. Also, Madam, you have a personal training session booked for this afternoon, and thalassotherapy later this evening."

"Thank you," I said. "See you in a few minutes."

Juan pulled himself up onto his elbows and gave me a look of sleepy confusion. "See who in a few minutes?"

"I'm supposed to be at a nutrition lecture that starts in 10 minutes. I didn't even know I had one. I must read all those notes they gave me when I checked in yesterday. Are you coming?"

"How can I? I'm not supposed to be here. I'm disguised, remember."

"But, do you want to come?"

"Yes," he said. "I guess so."

I rang reception and told them I'd like to bring a photographer along with me.

"He's flown over from England and is one of the most experienced and highly regarded photographers in the country," I assured them.

"I'm a photographer now? Without a camera?" said Juan.

"Yep."

"So, I just use my imaginary, invisible camera?"

"Improvise, my lovely," I said. "Use your phone, and take my laptop and pretend to download them or something. I don't know...what do photographers do? Now, come on, or we're going to be late."

Juan had a tendency to mutter to himself in his native Spanish when he was under pressure, and this time was no exception. I'd no idea what he was saying, but I was pretty sure that I didn't come out of it in a good light.

By the time we left the room we were already 10 minutes late for the lecture. Just outside the door lay a white envelope, addressed to: "Handsome man in purple hat."

I handed the letter to Juan.

"Is it from reception?" I asked, as he opened it, far too slowly for my liking. I'm much more of a 'rip it open' kind of girl. He was very much a 'delicately sliding your finger into the seal and taking the letter out, leaving the envelope looking pristine' sort of guy.

"It's a love letter," he said. "From the fitness guy."

I grabbed the letter off him and read it as we walked towards reception. "Dear handsome boy, I know you stay in Mary's room. Would you like to meet? I think we might have a lot in common... Maybe drinks tonight, while Mary is in dinner? M xxx"

"How does he know you might have a lot in common?" I asked. "He only glanced at you from a distance, and you were ducking and diving out of his way."

"By 'in common' I guess he means gay," said Juan.

"Is that a kind of code thing?"

"Not really, but what else could he mean?"

Juan tucked the envelope into his sports bag which contained my laptop and some male grooming tools - some odd metal instruments for squeezing blackheads, nail clippers and some device for removing hair from ears and noses. He planned to use this collection of things to persuade the PR department of an Italian hotel that he was a leading photographer.

"Are you going to reply to him?"

"I don't know. I want to. Would it be terrible if I did?"

"Of course not," I said. "But first you must pretend to be a leading photographer."

"Yeah, about that...what shall I do?"

"Just wander round and take pictures on your phone or something," I said, as we walked into the golf club and were directed to a large, well-appointed kitchen.

I sat down on a stool next to the cooking area and felt like Holly Willoughby on the cooking segments on This Morning. "So, Gino, what do you have for us today?' I said, offering a Willoughby-style megawatt smile. I thought I was being funny, but my comment just served to completely confuse things.

"My name is not Gino," he said, and immediately wanted to know who this Gino character was.

As I explained about This Morning, and all the various characters on it, I looked up to catch Juan's eye, but he was too busy doing imaginary measurements of the light in the room with a pencil, ear nose hair remover and the back of his iPhone. Eventually he nodded and announced that the light was right.

While my photographer snapped away, I was given a range of dazzlingly beautiful foods to try, all of them healthy but dripping in flavour.

"The more flavour in the food, and the more goodness the food - the less you will need of it, and the fuller you will feel," he said. "Eat burgers and pies and you'll never feel full, eat some really healthy, fresh, organic and well-cooked food and you will feel full in an instant. I promise you, that is the secret of healthy eating and why so many European women are slimmer than the British and American women."

I quite liked this 'eat lots of healthy flavours' business. Perhaps it was the notion of 'eat lots' that chimed with me. Flavia had said yesterday that everything served here came from within 1km of the Massaria. She had emphasised the importance the Italians attached to eating seasonal foods that were locally produced.

Eating good local produce had to be the best thing. The Italians drank wine made locally and they made their own olive oil. She said the most important thing was that they knew the derivation of everything they cooked or put on the table. They knew the person that grew or reared what we were eating. It meant that we were only putting into our mouths food that they could guarantee was full of goodness. Perhaps I should start growing my own food or something?

After the nutrition lesson, I was invited to take a seat while

Juan continued to capture photographs of the place, but I sensed that a minor rebellion was brewing.

"I don't want to take any more imaginary photographs," he whispered. "I feel a fool. They are looking at me as though there is something wrong with me as I walk around the room holding my pencil up to the light."

"Juan and his magic light pencil. It sounds like a children's book."

"Great. Now I am starring in my own weird, childish adventure. Can we go soon?"

CHAPTER SEVEN

*A*fter a few more imaginary photographs had been taken, Juan and I were guided to a rather formal looking table and chairs, given cups of coffee and told to relax while we waited for someone to come and show us round. Neither of us had any idea why we needed to be shown round; we had no interest at all in the place. But I was on a free trip, and I'd learned that the downside of taking these free holidays was that you were expected to be inordinately interested in all the details of the place. Behind us there was a large mirror reflecting the light of chandeliers above us. It made it all very sparkly and pretty.

Seeing a mirror reminded me of last night. I looked at Juan and saw the smile on his face. I realised he was thinking exactly the same thing: my conversation with my imaginary friend.

"Oh look," he said. "The drunk woman from the wedding reception has followed us here. Aren't you going to say hello?"

"Ha ha, you're hysterical," I said. "That was the old me. The new me is tee-total, vibrant and lovely at the spa."

A waitress brought a large bowl of fruit and an enormous plate of pastries to the table. "Your guide will be here soon," she said, then she turned to Juan: "You can take beautiful photographs of the golf club."

Juan nodded, and smiled.

"Good job you've got your magic pencil with you," I said, as he kicked me sharply under the table.

I hadn't eaten since lunchtime yesterday, but - most oddly - I wasn't hungry. The days of eating toast, cheese and crisps for breakfast appeared to be over. Juan took a large almond pastry and bit into it with gusto. I saw his eyebrows raise as I reached for an apple.

"I'm not hungry," I said, almost defensively. "Isn't it odd? I'm always hungry."

"Very odd," he agreed. "I'm completely bloody starving. It's almost lunchtime and we've had no breakfast."

While Juan munched his way through sweet, Italian pastries, I ate about half the apple then nipped out to the loo before we went on our walk about.

I went into the heavily-decorated cubicle and did what one must do. Then I tried to leave. I pushed and shoved but the door wouldn't budge.

Bugger.

I bashed the lock and wriggled it and leaned my weight against it. I shouted out but there was no one there so I put the lid on the toilet and sat down. I didn't know what to do.

I didn't have my phone on me to call for help, and I had no idea when anyone else would come in. Then I spotted it...a window by the side of me. It was quite small (and I'm quite large, in case you need reminding) but, nevertheless it was an escape route and given the absence of any other route, I knew I had to try. I clambered onto the toilet seat, and felt it give a little beneath me...sort of bow a little. Either I was going to get jammed in the window, or the seat was going to break, leaving me standing in the loo. Neither option was ideal, to be fair.

I reached up, and eased open the window. It wasn't high, but getting through it would involve a level of gymnastics that I wasn't convinced I could muster. I pushed myself through so that my head and shoulders were outside, and my legs inside. 'Half way' I reassured myself.

It turned out that the second half of the manoeuvre was more complicated. I kind of jigged myself forward so that most of my body was out of the window.

A smartly dressed golfer passed by outside and wished me good morning in Italian without stopping to think for a minute about what on earth I might be doing, hanging out of the window like that.

I shouted out to him to fetch me some help, but he just saluted and went on his way.

There was something very depressing about clambering out of the window - not just the very fact of being reduced to doing it in the first place, but also - how I can I put this delicately? - the very awful way in which my fat stomach was separated by the window...half of my fat hanging down one side, the other half hanging down the other. Don't mention this to anyone. I'm revealing it only so you will understand what an extraordinarily awful situation I was in.

It was like I needed someone to come along and hold my stomach up out of the way so I could slither out of the window. But if there were someone around, I'm not sure that I would have the guts to ask them to do such a horrible task, and I certainly didn't know the words to ask them in Italian.

So, I wriggled through, inch by inch, until the balance of my weight forced me to tip, then fall with a distinct lack of grace, straight through the window. I landed with an almighty thump outside. I was muddy and slightly disoriented but free from my toilet prison.

Juan was still sitting at the table and chairs when I ran around the hotel and back into the main reception area. He was looking intently at an Italian newspaper that I knew he couldn't read.

"Anything interesting?" I asked.

"Just reading about the financial markets in Ital... what the hell, Mary?"

"What?"

"You went to the loo, spent about half an hour there and have come back through a different door, looking like you've just played a game of rugby."

I looked down at my filthy clothing.

"Slight difficulty. I couldn't get out through the toilet door. I ended up climbing through the window and fell into the mud. No biggie."

CHAPTER EIGHT

"*E*xcuse me," said Juan, signalling flamboyantly to the waiter in a manner that was just on the right side of arrogant. "We have a little problem. My friend slipped over and we must go and change."

"Of course," said the woman, eyebrows raised as she took in the mud all over me. "Shall we meet you here when you are ready?"

"There's no need to give us a tour. We can take a look around ourselves, if that's OK?"

"Sure. Let me know if you need anything."

I changed quickly. I'd brought so few clothes with me because I woke up so late and hadn't packed, and many of the clothes simply didn't go together, so my options were limited.

"Fancy a wander," said Juan, when I emerged, clean and fresh. "Then you can run over the story again. I particularly like the detail about the guy stopping to tip his hat to you and wish you a good morning without noticing that you were hanging out of a window and completely stuck."

"Yep. That's exactly what happened. Now then, what do you fancy doing. Shall we head 'the quarter'.' This was the name for the villagey area situated between the three Massaria - our Massaria Blanca which was a spa hotel, a rather more corporate hotel called Masseria Raffinato and another one which was ideal for families with young children called Massaria Famigli. In the middle was 'the quarter' - a large courtyard full of shops, bars and restaurants that guests in any of the hotels could use.

"Yes. I really want to get a birthday present for Charlie," I said. "Something very classy and Italian."

We headed through the square which was laid out in a labyrinth of lanes with cobbled streets in search of such a gift. It was gorgeous; so Italian, with lots of little shops that specialised in one thing. I loved that. The big American malls are fun - you can go in and find all sorts of different things, all under one roof. But these dainty little Italian shops, owned by real craftsmen and women who knew everything about one subject: they were fab.

There was a lovely leather shop featuring a guy working with leather to make the handbags in the corner. We stopped a while and watched him tenderly pressing the leather until it was exactly the shape he wanted. The shop assistant let us stand and observe in silence without interrupting. There was no pressure to look at the merchandise; no pressure to buy. Yet, seeing the craftsman at work made me want to find something to take away. Something made by a genuine craftsman. Then I saw it; something that would be absolutely perfect for Charlie; a stunning leather handbag. It probably cost a fortune, but I had to take a look, so I marched Juan over to it, and together we oooh-ed and ahhh-ed at the softness of the leather and the intricacy of the stitching.

"I want to get it," I said.

"It's £300," said Juan. "That's a lot of money."

"You are hotel guest?" said the assistant.

"Yes."

"You have 25% off all purchases."

"Oh My God. I have to get it," I said to Juan. "She would love it."

"I'll get the purse and make up bag to match," said Juan, laying the two items next to the handbag.

"They look great," I said. "Come on, let's do this."

After our handbag shopping, we stopped at a beautiful boutique selling handmade Italian gloves - made to measure - but they really were too expensive to buy from, then passed the most delicious cake shop emitting such glorious smells that we both stopped in our tracks and stood, heads up, sniffing the air.

"Lunch?" we said in unison...the smell of bread and cakes was all too much for us to bear.

Juan approached a waiter and asked for us to be seated outside a pasta restaurant next to the bakery.

But something had distracted me.

"Oh my God - look," I said, staring at the clothes shop in front of us. "Will you look at that..."

In the window of a shop called 'Bella Bella' was a beautiful, floor-length, red dress. It sat elegantly across the shoulders of the model in the window and fell to the floor. "I've never seen a dress so beautiful in my life before," I cried, practically dragging Juan away from the waiter and into the shop.

The assistant smiled at me as I asked to see the dress. It was too small to try on, of course, but I held it up in front of me and looked at myself in the mirror and knew that I had to have a dress like that for Charlie's party. The label had no price on it, so I knew it was way out of my range.

"Take a picture of me," I said, thrusting my phone into Juan's hand, and holding it back up in front of me again.

"It's called Pretty Lady," said the assistant. "The colour is suit you."

I DIDN'T KNOW WHETHER IT WAS SEEING THE DRESS, AND thinking about Charlie's party, or whether it was just the fact that I wasn't eating very much and exercising a lot, but I hit a real low point after our shopping trip, and felt sadder than ever that evening, and completely exhausted. I lay on the bed, looking at Juan, until tears began running down my face. I'd worked hard in my personal training session and enjoyed thalassotherapy. I'd felt uplifted afterwards. But now, here I was, almost bereft.

"It's bloody hopeless," I said to Juan. "He's with Dawn and there's nothing I can do about it. He's bound to fall head over heels in love with her and that will be the end of Ted and me. The end of everything. I'll be alone for the rest of my life."

"Oh angel, that's not going to happen. Why don't you send him a quick text, or drop him an email or something?"

"Because he's got a girlfriend. It's over. Finito."

"She's not a girlfriend. He was seen out with her once. Just once. You went on a whole load of dates after Ted. You wouldn't call every guy you went out with a boyfriend, would you?"

"No."

"So, why are you assuming they are boyfriend and girlfriend?"

"Because Dawn said they were."

"Oh, ignore her. She's always been strange, that one. I've never liked her."

"I feel so sad."

"I know you do. Come here." Juan hugged me as I cried into his shoulder. He held me tightly and we stayed there, wrapped up together in complete silence. It felt like we could have stayed there forever until I heard a knock on the door. I had no desire to answer it looking like such a state. I shouted instead: "Hello, can I help you?"

"It's Marco here. I have come to meet your friend. Also, I have a letter for you."

"Could you push the letter underneath?" I asked, turning to Juan and mouthing: "Do you want to see him?"

Juan shrugged, but I could see by the look on his face that he did.

"You can go, I'll be fine," I said, retrieving the letter which appeared at my feet.

"You are invited to lunch at 12pm with Eva Bianca, the owner of the Massaria."

"Get you," said Juan. "So posh!"

"Go on, go for a drink with Marco, and I'll see you later," I said, easing the door open and pushing him through it. "Have fun."

I sat down on the bed after Juan had gone, and googled the owner's name.

My search revealed that Eva Massaria was one of the richest women in Italy....from an aristocratic family. She owned eight

Massaria in southern Italy, including the three that were based here, in Bari.

As I googled my way through her life, clicking on 'translate' to guide me through the articles in the local newspapers I learnt all about the woman who had come from poverty to build up this amazing business. Next, I googled her husband. He died three years ago but looked very debonair and handsome in the pictures. He had been in the military for most of his life but joined his wife to manage the Massaria after retiring. This lunch could be interesting.

Then another thought came to me. I wonder what would happen if I put Dawn Baxter's name into google. I wonder what it would tell me about my love rival.

There was very little about her at all. Though there's not much on me, to be honest. The details of her Facebook account came up, and I clicked onto it, but she was one of those people who kept it all secure, so I couldn't get far. I needed to find out whether she had posted pictures of her and Ted. Had she changed her status update? But the last thing I wanted to do was send her a friend request.

That's when it came to me. I needed to set up a different Facebook account, with a different name, and send Dawn a friend request from that one. That way I could spy on her without her realising she was being monitored.

Genius.

There was something exciting and invigorating about being underhand. It distracted me from thoughts of Ted and my mood had lifted greatly. I assembled pictures for my new persona. I decided I'd have quite a big family because I'd liked to have had brothers and sisters when I was growing up. And I gave myself a dog called Kettle (I know, I know - but I couldn't think of a name and the first thing I saw when I looked up was the kettle).

Once my page was complete, I began befriending everyone on Dawn's friends list, in the hope that some would follow me back, so that by the time Dawn read my friend request she would see that we had many mutual friends and thus be more inclined to accept mine.

I'd just sent out a second batch of friend requests when there was a gentle tap on the door. I opened it cautiously to see Juan standing there.

"Let me in and lock the door. The man's insane," he said.

"What's happened?"

"He kept grabbing me and stroking me and saying he thought he was falling in love with me. I don't know what's wrong with him."

"Oh my God - really?"

"Yes. It was like he'd never been on a date before. I told him to calm down and stop touching me, but he wouldn't listen. Three times I warned him. Three times. I stayed for one drink then rushed back. Hey, what's this?"

He was looking at the laptop that I had unwisely left open on the bed.

"Who is Barbara Moffett?"

"A friend," I said, trying to take the computer off him.

"But you're in her Facebook page like it's your own. How did you do that? What are you up to, Mary?"

"Nothing."

"You're up to something."

"I created a false profile," I said.

"Why?"

"So I could befriend Dawn. Her account is all private, the

only thing I can see is her list of friends. I wanted to see whether she had changed her status on there, and see whether she had posted any pictures of herself with Ted.

Juan took the computer from me and put it down on the floor.

"Come here," he said, taking me into his arms. "I'm going to cuddle you while you fall asleep."

CHAPTER NINE

*E*va Massaria, owner of the hotel complex, looked exactly as I knew she would... subtly elegant with thick hair moulded into a bob, coloured a flattering light golden brown... you know the colour? Only the Italians have it. It's a sort of caramel with buttery highlights: unimaginably glossy and sophisticated. I don't know how they get their hair like that: it must be a state secret or something. All I knew, as I approached her, was that I was very envious, even though she must have had a good 50 years on me.

She was slim, of course, and well-dressed Italian-style – suede loafers, elegantly tailored cream trousers, a white blouse and a camel coloured suede jacket over her shoulders. She had gold earrings (obviously real - I'd never seen anything like those in Clair's accessories), and a handbag by Gucci which screamed 'I am very rich, very stylish and very elegant get out of my goddamn way.'

I, on the other hand, was not dressed like that.

Let me explain...do you remember that I mentioned how badly I'd packed to come away? Well that, added to the fact that I was in a giant rush to get ready, had made it all go wrong.

I had on a little summer dress which didn't quite fit across the chest, so the top button kept bursting open. In order to remedy this, I had put a scarf around my neck. No one needed to be greeted by the sight of my breasts bouncing free. It wasn't a very warm day so I put on a pair of leggings underneath. This was done for warmth rather than sartorial reasons. I looked like I'd been dressed in a jumble sale

I should add that I had my trainers on with this unlikely get-up, and my trainers were the brightest orange. I couldn't wear them without socks or I got blisters, but – because this is me – I'd only managed to bring black socks with me, so I had black socks, orange trainers, purple leggings, an ill-fitting summer dress in a red floral pattern and a yellow scarf. It was like I'd deliberately tried to incorporate every pattern and every colour under the sun.

Then there was my handbag which was pink, and I wore large sunglasses which were added at the last minute, and designed to give me a degree of style. Basically, I was hoping to distract her from my truly terrible outfit by making my face resemble that of an oversized beetle.

Mrs Bianca didn't seem to be fazed at all by any of this. She smiled warmly and shook my hand before showing me into the restaurant and indicating where we would be sitting. As soon as we walked into the room it was as if the queen had walked in. I noticed the sly glances and the rushing around as everyone sought to ingratiate themselves. I guess that's what happens when you own the whole damn place.

She told me to take a seat while she wafted through the restaurant, glad-handing everyone.

A waiter rushed over to the table to ask me what I'd like to drink. It didn't feel right to order a diet coke or a beer or anything. Despite my outfit, I did know how to conduct myself in polite company, so I ordered a large bottle of still water. No one in the world could have any complaints about still water, could they?

Mrs Bianca came back and slipped into the seat opposite me, lifting up her glass and pushing it gently towards her lips. But as soon as she tasted the water she howled and dropped her glass, her eyebrows reaching up into the recesses of her hair line. It was like she had drunk poison. She put down the glass and swung her arm in the air to call the waiters over. Predictably enough, they arrived by the dozen. She said something in Italian and there were gasps and the glasses taken away.

"Is there a problem?" I asked. Perhaps her class had a chip in it, or there was some terrible stain on it.

"It was still water," she said, spelling out the words clearly and aggressively. "They bring me still water."

It turned out that madam drank nothing but sparkling water. She couldn't abide tea or coffee, had never let an alcoholic drink past her neatly made up lips, and certainly did not drink still water. "What were they thinking?"

"I'm sorry, I ordered the still water," I said. "It's my fault."

"Oh. You like still water?" It was as if she'd asked me whether I liked to drink the blood of goats. In all honesty I wasn't not all that bothered what sort of water I drank. Was anyone except Mrs Bianca?

"I don't mind what water."

"Then why you order still?"

"I thought you would like still water," I said. "You look so lovely and sophisticated and I thought you must take care of yourself, so I thought I'd order still."

I don't know what happened at that point...whether it was the awkwardness I'd created, her anger or a general disappointment in myself, but I burst into tears.

She looked at me for a moment. "You would like the still water?"

"No, it's not about the water. I'm just a bit sad," I said.

With that, she softened.

Her suddenly gentler demeanour was all it took to start me off, and I really burst into tears. I mean properly crying. She looked horrified, glancing around for someone to help her to manage the complicated situation that had suddenly developed with the overweight, ridiculously-dressed Englishwoman. The waiters weren't sure how to react either, so they put the still water back on the table, and retreated quickly. She handed me a white handkerchief with her initials sewn in violet in the corner. I was dying to blow my nose, but I knew I couldn't, so I dabbed at my eyes in as graceful a way as I could.

"I'm sorry," I sobbed at her, snorting indelicately. "I've just had such a difficult time. My ex-boyfriend who I really love is going out with someone else and I can't believe it. I'm so sorry. This is very unprofessional of me."

Eva smiled, and instructed me to tell her everything. She might have wished she hadn't asked, because I did. I told her every last detail. I told her about Dawn and how I didn't want to be fat anymore and had seen such a lovely red dress in

BonBon, and how I wanted to impress him at the party, but it was all so hard.

I explained that the party was in just over five weeks, and I had so much weight to lose: how was I ever going to do it?

It was like chatting to an old friend who I always confided in. The only difference was that her English wasn't perfect so she misheard a couple of things. When I told her about the wonderful red dress, she thought I said 'west Indian headdress' so we went off on a bit of a tangent about why I wanted to dress like a chief. I had to show her the picture of me holding it out in front of me in order for her to understand, and stop patting her hand against her mouth to make that red Indian calling sound.

She, in turn, told me about her lovely late husband, and how much they had worked together over the years to build their hotel empire. She shed a few tears, I shed a lot of tears, and - honestly - by the end of it all I felt like I'd made a real friend. I wished I weren't going home the next day. I wanted to hang out with her a bit more.

"I'm sorry about my clothes," I said, sweeping my hand down the length of my body. I didn't bring the right things and I look so daft."

"You look perfect. I'm envious of your youth and spirit."

We hugged goodbye and promised to keep in touch, though I knew we probably wouldn't. I would definitely say lots of nice things about her on the blog.

"How did it go?" asked Juan when I got back to the room.

"I cried non-stop. It was fab," I replied.

"You cried non-stop? With the owner?"

"Yes, she didn't like still water, but I ordered still water and there was a big drama and…. Oh, you don't want to hear all this, but I ended up telling her all about Ted and me and how much I loved him."

"Oh angel," said Juan, gently stroking my hair.

"No, it was OK, honestly. I even gave her the date of the party and told her to come. That was a bit of a mistake. It's Charlie's 30th for her closest friends, I shouldn't be going around inviting random Italian billionaires.

We lay there on the bed for a little while, until the silence was brought to a dramatic end by a knock on the door.

"Oh God," said Juan, diving behind the bed. "If it's Marco, tell him I died."

When I opened the door, Flavia, the lovely hotel manager, was standing there.

"Hello," I said warmly. "How are you?"

"I am fine," she said, though she didn't sound fine at all. I hadn't seen her since our lunch on the first day; the happy, smiley lady with whom I'd shared soup and salad seemed to have been replaced by a thoroughly miserable, slightly angry-looking woman.

"Can I help you?"

"I hope so. Do you remember I told you about my fiancé? He works here in the hotel?"

"Yes, of course I remember. Is something wrong?"

"I'm sorry to have to ask, but I really need to know something."

"Sure," I said. "Just ask away."

"Are you having an affair with him?"

"What? I haven't even met him."

"Yes, you have met him. He ran your classes and he comes over here all the time. I saw on the hotel CCTV. Marco. You do know him."

I heard a small squeak from behind the bed.

"Marco. The fitness guy? Yes. Sorry, I know him. He is your fiancé?"

"Are you having an affair with him?"

I just looked at her blankly, but Flavia looked deadly serious.

"No, of course not."

"I can hear someone in the room. Is it Marco?"

"No, of course not."

"Yes, I heard someone. Marco is here. How could you?"

"No, no, no... you've got this all wrong," I said. "This is completely wrong."

"You went out with him last night, didn't you? I knew he was lying. You have been having an affair."

"No, she hasn't," came a voice from inside the room. Flavia and I both turned. "She hasn't been having an affair with him. I went out for a drink with him last night but we're not having an affair."

Juan stood there with his hands on his hips like he was prepared to take on all-comers to protect my reputation.

"You need to talk to Marco, not come shouting accusations at my friend."

"I'm sorry," said Flavia, now addressing Juan, rather than me. "I'd prefer it if you wouldn't encourage him."

"No one is encouraging him, I can assure you," said Juan. "As I said - go and talk to him."

I closed the door and looked over at Juan.

"Do you really think she doesn't know he's gay?"

"She must do," he agreed. "She told me not to encourage him, so she must know something's not right."

"You know, matey, I think it's a good job we're going home tomorrow."

"Agreed," he said. "And - for the record - Marco is very gay. Very gay indeed."

I checked my phone before going to bed that night and saw there was a message from Facebook. "Dawn Baxter has accepted your friend request," it said.

CHAPTER TEN

I got the feeling that Juan was glad to be out of Italy. It was the way in which he punched the air triumphantly and squealed with delight as our plane lifted off the ground that gave it away.

"The weirdest experience," he was saying to himself, while smiling with relief. "I never felt quite safe in that hotel, you know. I didn't like hiding, I didn't like pretending to be a photographer, and I was chatted up the gayest man in the world. A man who was way too gay for my tastes, then it turns out he has a fiancé who is manager of the whole place and who became convinced that you were having an affair with him."

"Yeah - pretty bonkers," I replied.

"He kept appearing wherever I was, and putting letters through the door. I'd love to know what was going on in his silly head."

"You can ask him," I replied, pointing towards the front of the plane. "There he is. It's Marco. Right there..."

I swear to God, I don't think I'd ever seen Juan look more frightened. He dropped down in his seat until he was squashed into the foot well.

"I'm joking," I said. "Just a little joke."

"It's too serious to joke about, honestly," he said, unravelling himself and clambering back into his seat. "That guy had no idea whether he wanted an Arthur or a Martha. I was lucky to escape with my life."

"Thank you for coming out to see me, though, it really cheered me up."

"Thank you for being the best friend in the world. You rescued me. You let me live with you...in your little flat. You are so kind. Love you," he said.

I smiled at Juan, and felt very lucky. It was heart-breaking that I'd lost my boyfriend, but heart-warming to have such a lovely friend.

That night I snuggled up in my own bed and felt pleased to be back. I'm not saying I didn't enjoy my three-day trip, but it had been odd to be away when I felt so sad about Ted.

I pulled out my phone to do something I'd been dying to do all day...look through Dawn's Facebook page and see whether there was any mention of Ted. I put in my fake details and Dawn's face filled the screen. She had some sort of face paint on and looked like she was at a music festival or something. I never saw her as being the music festival type, but there she was - shaking her stuff with a rainbow painted across her nose and cheeks and glitter in her hair.

The first thing I looked at, of course, was her status. It didn't say that she was in a relationship. Phew! Excellent, excellent. This was all looking good. I scrolled down through her timeline and saw nothing that related to Ted in any way. There was all the usual stuff - her out with the girls, her on all her holidays, a few pictures of food she'd cooked and some of those messages people post from time to time, warning that Facebook must not steal their photos or messages or anything. That was it. The great thing was that I could now keep an eye on her, and see whether any pictures appeared of Ted and her. I knew there was a very real danger that I was going to become obsessed, and checking out her social media pages constantly, but at least I'd know what was going on. I fell asleep that night feeling relieved and happier than I had for a while.

THE NEXT DAY, IT WAS STRAIGHT BACK TO WORK, AND I WAS faced with the task of moving all the pot plants around in the nursery for no good reason other than Keith, my boss, had decided the shop floor needed a face lift. Christ alive, it was tough work. There was a forklift truck that was available for me to use, but - you know what I'm like - I can't drive a car and am chaotic at the best of times. Letting me loose with a truck with a huge fork on the front would most certainly end in loads of smashed plants, and probably a couple of seriously injured customers. As a result, I was reduced to carrying the Styrofoam containers full of plants over to the other side of the huge centre. Because I wasn't very strong, I had to take them one at a time, and it was taking forever.

Barry was helping me, but he was useless. He was usually on hardware, but after an unfortunate incident with a box of taps on the edge of a high shelf and an elderly lady's dog, he was moved onto general duties. He wasn't allowed to work alone, so I had to accompany him at all times. After half an hour, I could see why - he kept dropping things, taking things to the wrong place and generally being useless.

It was all a bit much to cope with after doing nothing but lounge around in an Italian hotel for the last few days. But as well as keeping a close eye on Barry, I was determined to carry on with all the good work I'd done in Italy and continue to lose weight. I knew that while I'd been away I had eaten way, way less than I normally did, and I was desperate to keep up the low calorie, all-natural, healthy eating. The trouble was - how? We didn't have olive trees in the garden. Hell - I didn't even have a garden. There weren't spreads of delicious fruits every morning, just waiting for me in the dining room, and there were no big jugs of lemon and lime water placed around the place for whenever I got thirsty.

Juan had insisted that I could replicate much of what I'd seen in Italy by going to the health food shop and the market and buying a load of fresh produce, but I knew that strategy wouldn't work for long: it was too high maintenance. I'd love to be the girl in every French film who is walking along with a basket teeming with bunches of freshly picked mint and basil, on her arm, but in reality, I knew I couldn't be arsed with all that. I needed something easier - something straight forward, simple to follow, but guaranteed to work.

I had read in a magazine about the Spoon Diet: an eating programme in which you could eat anything you like: soup, yogurt, pudding - anything. Sounds good so far, doesn't it? The only thing was that you had to eat it all with a teaspoon. It meant that a bowl of soup took an hour to eat, and apple crumble and custard filled up the whole evening. It was hard to eat burgers and pizzas, but fruit salad was straight forward. So, that morning I had decided to give it a go, and had confidently headed for work with a teaspoon tucked into my handbag.

By the time I finished the day I was in a huge sulk. It had been dismal. Instead of eating slowly and cherishing every morsel, as they had advised at the spa, I found myself shovelling food into my mouth at record-breaking speed in order to eat enough in my lunch hour to keep me full. Also, I found myself paying no heed as to whether food was healthy or not; I just ate what I could fit onto a spoon. By the end of the day I realised that my main consumption that day had been chocolate mousse, peanut butter, jelly and yoghurt. I'm sure I was above the recommended calories for the day while lacking in every essential nutrient. I treated myself to an apple that evening that I would never have been able to eat with a teaspoon, and had an early night. I continued with my efforts to lose weight the 'teaspoon way' for the rest of the week, but it was driving me nuts.

"I've made a huge decision about my life," I said to Juan and Charlie a week or so later.

"What?" asked Juan, digging into his regular morning porridge before his six Pilates classes (he teaches six in a day! I can't do one).

I held up a dessert spoon as a clue. "I'm giving up the tiny teaspoon diet."

"Oh good," they chorused. "That's a bloody relief. I think fad diets are a waste of... Hang on, what's that?"

I held in front of me a book, with 'South Beach Diet' printed across the cover. "This, my friend, is going to be the key to thinness."

"Really? Why don't you just eat wholesome food and get some exercise - the weight will fly off you."

"Nope. This is the diet for me. All the celebs love it. There are three phases to it: I have to start with lean proteins, vegetables, and nuts. No carbs or sugar. Then I add some grains back in during phase two, then in phase three I can eat like a normal human being, but a healthy human being."

"Sweetheart, you don't need to do all this crap. I know all about diet and fitness. I'll help you choose healthy foods, and take you to my Pilates classes and I promise your life will be transformed."

"I know this is the diet for me," I said, holding the book to my heart and rocking gently, as if soothing a crying baby. "Through this plan I will lose loads of weight and look utterly adorable."

"Well, when you're fed up of the silly weight loss plans, let me know and I'll show you how to do it the Pilates way."

"Yeah, OK."

"Haven't you two got someone on this morning?"

"Yes, we've got party planning to do. I want Charlie's 30th to be the best party in the world."

"Enjoy," said Juan. "Mary - the diet won't work. Don't overdo it. I'll be watching you...."

I hoped that Juan wasn't watching too closely over the next few weeks, as I tried desperately to relish the celery and carrots I was forced to eat in place of proper food. It wasn't a clever or interesting diet; it was a weight loss programme on which you lost weight because you weren't allowed to eat anything. I felt weaker and weaker as the days and weeks went on, going to bed early to avoid eating in the evenings, and even resorting to chewing on cotton wool to try to ease the hunger pains. It was horrific. I vowed to get myself to the weekend, then I'd stop it. I swear to God, Friday evening could not come fast enough.

CHAPTER ELEVEN

*I*t was just two weeks until the party, and I felt torn as I thought about the prospect of seeing Ted again. Torn because I knew that he would either walk in with Dawn and it was all over, or walk in alone, come up to me and talk to me. At the moment I was able to fantasise about the party and what might happen. I was able to cheer myself up by looking at her Facebook page and concluding that no sign of Ted on there meant they weren't having much of a relationship. Even if Dawn had been honest when she said that she'd been seeing Ted, that could be over now. That was a few weeks ago. They might have been for a few drinks, then called it a day.

The trouble was, the fantasies would stop when the party came around, because then I'd know for good. I couldn't play out scenarios in my mind to make me feel happy and hopeful...the real thing would be here, and if it wasn't what I wanted, I knew I'd be doubly sad; because I wasn't back with Ted, and the hope of getting back with Ted would be gone. It was the hope that was keeping me going at the moment.

I looked at the alarm clock by my bed...it was 8am. On a Saturday morning. And I was wide awake. This was unheard of. I have to confess that the main reason I was up so early was because I was dying to go to the loo, I'll spare you the details, but these diets I've been on have been playing absolute havoc with my system, but also because I needed to write the blog about my trip to Italy before Dawn had to call me and tell me it was late. I didn't want any contact from her at all. The blog was due to go up on the site on Monday. I'd almost finished it, but I wanted to read it through and check it was OK.

I called it up on my laptop and studied the words.

"The owner is beautiful, kind and easy-to-talk-to," I'd written. "She presides over a hotel empire that embodies all of her fine characteristics..."

I hoped she would see what I'd written. I'd love her to realise how great I thought she was. Perhaps I should send her a note? Oh God - I should definitely have done that. I should have bought her a nice card, and sent it to her. Why did I think of these things so far after the event?

I put up my blog post onto the Two Fat Ladies site along with pictures I'd taken of the hotel, and a lovely one of Eva that I found online, then decided to head right out, there and then, to get her a thank you card. It was better to send one late than to never send one at all. I threw on a pair of jeans which felt remarkably loose. Alleluja! I must have lost quite a lot for them to feel that baggy. Then I put on an old sweatshirt and trainers and walked out to the corner shop where I bought a book of stamps and a card, then I walked down to the river to sit and write it. I ended up producing quite an essay for Eva...I told her all about the various diets I'd tried to go on for the party in two weeks' time, and updated her on Ted and how I was friends with Dawn on Facebook, and Dawn hadn't posted anything about Ted (I left out the part about me having created a whole new persona to lure Dawn in, and was using the social media platform to spy on her). I pushed the card into the envelope and wrote the address of the hotel on it. Then, because I had no idea how much the postage to Italy was, I took every stamp from the book and put them all on, then I walked over to the post box to send it on its way to Masseria Bianca.

It was such a lovely day that it seemed a shame to go back inside. If I returned to the flat before Juan was up, I'd just end up eating my bodyweight in breakfasty things. Instead, I decided to go for a sharp stroll around before everyone got up, then I could return feeling virtuous and wonderful. OK, maybe not wonderful...I wasn't planning to break the Olympic record or anything, but a stroll around the block was better than going home and eating a bacon and crisp sandwich (note to readers: for the avoidance of doubt - a walk is better than a bacon and crisp sandwich only in terms of weight loss... in all other respects a bacon sandwich trumps exercise of any kind, every day).

So, I strolled down the road, pumping my arms as I went, trying to increase my speed and get my blood flowing. I could feel my body using up all those fat molecules so generously spread across my body as I powered through the quiet streets of Cobham. I remembered the words of the military trainer who'd been leading the weight loss camp I went on a few years ago. He had told me to pump my arms as fast as possible when I walked, because that would make me walk faster. Well the way I was pumping them this morning, I could have beaten Usain Bolt in a race.

The trouble was, arm pumping and walking fast was surprisingly tiring. I'd done about 10 minutes at top speed - power wiggling along with arms moving like pistons and felt worse than most people do after a marathon. Ahead of me was the church near the main road into the centre of Cobham. I would speed walk as far as there, then have a little break.

I had never really noticed the church before. I mean, I knew it was there, I'm not stupid, but I'd never realised how lovely it was, with its tall spire lifting up into the sky, and the magnificence of the building. And the beautiful stained-glass windows. The colours in them seemed so vibrant...an extraordinary peacock blue and ruby red. It was dazzling. How could it be just 10 minutes from my flat, and be something I had never noticed. I was captivated...I needed to take a closer look.

I walked up the wonky path towards the front door, feeling like a bride on her wedding day about to enter the church. Are you allowed to just walk into churches? I sort of hovered by the door, not sure whether I could just walk in. Perhaps there were certain times of day when they were open? So many questions... I tried the handle on the door and felt it move slightly in my hand as if it was about to allow entry, but when I pushed a little harder, it didn't shift at all. The whole door was bolted from within. Perhaps there was another way to get inside? I walked back out along the path, and round to the side, where the stained-glass windows looked even more magnificent, gleaming in the early morning sun. There was an entrance on the other side of the church, not as magnificent as the main entrance, just a little path up to a more homely-looking small wooden door next to a noticeboard. There were notes on there about various parish events that were taking place. I looked through the services on offer to see whether there was any indication of opening and closing times (sorry - I know that sounds a bit like a pub, but you get my drift.)

On the board there were details about a Sunday school, bible reading, flower arranging lessons and a children's playgroup every Wednesday night. Then, on the left-hand side was something far more interesting - a mindfulness course being run in the church hall: "Six weeks to transform your thinking and make you feel better than ever." That sounded like the sort of thing I needed. Something to drag me out of my misery about Ted, and get me smiling again. I pulled out my phone and took a picture of the noticeboard. I would email the woman and see whether I could join the course starting in two months' time. Then I noticed a piece of paper pinned on with a solitary drawing pin, flapping in the gentle breeze.

The sign said: "Leading Psychic, sessions available this week. Learn what the future holds for you."

Wow. That sounded exciting. I love a psychic. I'd been to a few in my time. Nothing they said to me has ever remotely come true, but it's such great fun seeing what they have to say. Perhaps this one would be the key to a happy life. Perhaps she could give me advice about Ted? Perhaps I would be set off on the right path. I mean, what could go wrong? She was advertising outside the church hall, for God sake. I mean, if she had been given the blessing of Christianity, surely I could trust her? I pulled out my phone again and took a picture of the name and number.

The marvellous Sheila... psychic and healer.

Now then, anyone tell me that doesn't sound like a kosher name for a psychic? Sheila the Healer. It was perfect. She even had a picture below of her, wearing a scarf and hoop earrings with her hands out over a mini ball from which electrical impulses were flying.

This was just what I needed. It was the way in which I was going to win the love of my life back. And maybe even give me the key to permanent lifelong weight loss along the way. She might be, in short, the answer to all my prayers. You see – it does pay to come to church.

"Thank you, God," I shouted up to the steeple as I walked away from the church, clutching my phone in my hand as I power-walked back home.

Later that day, I called Sheila and left a message on what sounded like a very business-like answering service. I had expected the message to be full of mystic sounds, perhaps coming from a distant world far away, but it just said very officiously: "Hello. Please speak after the tone. If you want to call me at work, I am now working for Elmbridge Council waste disposal department, so try me there."

I left a message. "Hello, I wanted to talk to Sheila, the psychic healer - but you probably know that! Ha ha. My name's Mary Brown. I guess you knew that too. Ha! Er, anyway, here's my number...call me."

Shit. Why did I say that? She must be sick to death of people saying 'but I guess you know that already.'

I rang up again.

"Hi Sheila, It's Mary again. Er, just wanted to say sorry about that message. Really stupid. Anyway...call me."

DESPITE THE INAUSPICIOUS STAR, I SOON RECEIVED A TEXT FROM Sheila, full of pictures of tarot cards and candles, inviting me to come for a reading at 3pm on Monday. It meant having to sneak out of work so I told Keith, my boss, that I had to go to a doctor's appointment.

"Why on earth would you schedule a doctor's appointment for 3 o'clock in the afternoon? Could you really not go in your lunchtime or after work?" he asked.

"Sorry. It's women's problems," I explained, seeing the look of terror on his face. "The only time I could get an appointment with a gynaecologist was at 3 o'clock. You see the problem with my ovaries is..." Keith raised his hand and shooed me away. "That's fine, Mary. No need for details."

I decided in that moment that whenever I needed anything, any time off, or any peace and quiet, I would roll out the women's problems line and be afforded all the time off I needed.

It turned out that Sheila's house was a rather plain looking place on a council estate on the other side of town. Kids who should have been at school raced bikes up and down the pavement while parents shouted from kitchen windows at them to stop. I stepped over an abandoned skateboard and walked up to Sheila's door, knocked it, and listened to the sound of a man and woman shouting at one another while a dog yapped.

It was at this point that it occurred to me that I really should have told someone where I was going. No one in the world knew that I'd come to talk to Sheila the Healer. The only person who knew I wasn't at work was Keith, and he thought I disappeared off to get women's problems sorted. They would have a hell of a job finding me if I was kidnapped. I took my phone out of my handbag and held it tightly as I knocked again.

A sloppy-looking man opened the door to me. He had a distinct potbelly and wore an ill-fitting football shirt for a team I didn't recognise, slightly stained jogging bottoms and was holding a small dog. "Sorry to disturb you. I've come to see Sheila," I said.

"Who?"

"Psychic Sheila? Sheila the healer?"

"Oh yes, come in."

"Margaret, there is someone at the door for you."

So, she lived in a scruffy house with a rough-looking man, she was going by a false name - she wasn't Sheila the healer at all, but Margaret from the waste disposal office at the council. It would be a lie to say that my confidence in her was at all all-time high. But I tried to reassure myself, it didn't mean she wasn't a good psychic.

I followed her husband along the corridor that was cluttered with shoes and coats, and into a sitting room that looked like everyone's mum's house. Perfectly nice and comfortable, but nothing terribly stylish or modern. The television in the corner was showing some sort of football game. The sound was turned up very loud. There was a sofa facing the tv and two armchairs by the side. In the middle there was a coffee table and on it the only clue as to who lived in the place... a magazine called "Psychic Today" next to a can of beer and one of those monster-sized bags of crisps.

"Come through," said a disembodied voice, emphasising the 'oooo' at the end of the word, to make it sound a little spooky. She needn't have worried about being more spooky - I was quite spooked enough already.

I walked from the sitting room into a small conservatory which led onto a small garden. It was decked out with fairy lights and candles and was much more like I'd imagined a psychic's house to be. I was guided to the seat opposite Sheila, with a small wooden table between us covered in a lacy table cloth. On it there was all the paraphernalia that one would associate with a psychic...some cards, candles, a notebook, a teapot and some sort of globe thing - like the one on the notice I'd seen at the church, but without the electric sparks coming out of it.

Sheila herself was nice...she had dyed blonde hair that was actually more yellow than blonde, drawn-on eyebrows that were nowhere near where her real eyebrows ought to be, and about four earrings in each ear. Her eyeshadow was in the same lilac as the curtains, but she had a very nice aura about her: a big smile which suggested a generous, kindly nature despite her efforts to look ethereal and distant. I felt immediately at ease.

She took my hands in hers. She had a lot of rings on her fingers and bangles on her wrists: all of them ugly. I assumed they all had incredible psychic powers, but the bangles jangled in an annoying fashion and were too big and tarnished to be attractive. She had a sort of gypsyish quality, but also was quite like a nurse or something...she had a solidly about her. I decided instantly that she would change my life.

"Derek," she screamed out through the open conservatory door. "Can you close the door, and turn the television down, I'm trying to do a reading."

There was a shuffling and then the banging of the door, and the sounds of football disappeared into the background. "What can I do for you, Mary?" she said softly. "What is it you're looking to get from today's session?"

CHAPTER TWELVE

"*I* would like some clues as to what the future holds," I said.

I was being wise. I knew that if I gave her lots of information about what was happening in my life, she would be able to convince me that she was psychic by gradually revealing it all back to me. I'd heard about all those dodgy psychics and their underhand ways.

"Hold my hand," said Sheila. I pushed my pudgy paws across the table, instantly wishing that I'd given myself a manicure. She lifted her chin in the air, eyes closed, as if beaming down information from a far-off universe; a universe which contained the answers to all my deepest questions.

"Sheila, did you get any dog food and poo bags?" came a voice, not from the universe but from the doorway where Sheila's husband Derek stood holding their tiny dog.

"Not now," said Sheila. "I'm looking into the future."

"I can tell you exactly what will happen in the future if you don't get poo bags. Tyson will shi..."

"OK, thank you, Derek. We all know what will happen."

The conservatory door was slammed shut, with the dog on our side of it. He ran across to Sheila and jumped into her lap, whining incessantly.

"This is no good," she said. "We will have to go and get dog food. Come on, I'll do you a reading in Asda."

I wasn't sure whether she was joking at this point, but as she pulled on a magnificent cloak which shined and sparkled with pictures of moons and stars, and threw a fabulous scarf around her neck, dotted with crystals, gold sparkles and fringes, it became clear that we were certainly going somewhere.

Sheila picked up a large bag that was also covered in moons and stars, but didn't in anyway match the rest of her outfit, threw the dog into it and instructed me to follow her.

"He just wants me out of the house," she said, as we drove along in her tiny, battered little car while I held Tyson. It was the sort of vehicle that you would imagine an 18-year-old boy driving when he'd just passed his driving test. The thing coughed and spluttered along the street, with Sheila becoming increasingly agitated as she struggled to change gear when her magnificent cloak wrapped itself around the gear stick in a very unmagnificent way.

It was a miracle, and a considerable relief, when she pulled into the Asda car park and parked next to the giant, industrial bins at the far side.

"You wait here," she said, kissing Tyson on the head. "Look after the dog while I get the food."

With that, she went striding through the car park, her crazy long coat trailing on the ground behind her while her scarf and crazy hair flew out like she was walking into a wind tunnel. She was a sparkly vision of well – madness – to be honest. As soon as she was out of sight, I put Tyson down on her seat, pulled my phone out of my bag and face timed Juan.

"I'm coming to you live from the Asda car park," I said, moving the phone round slowly so he could see the glamour of the environment.

"Lovely," he said. "So glad you called to tell me."

"I'm with a psychic called Sheila at the healer. Actually, that's not true. I'm with Sheila the healer's dog called Tyson, and Sheila the healer is actually called Margaret, and she is in the shop buying poo bags."

"I'm sure there's a good reason for all of this," said Juan. "But I'm struggling to think of it at the moment."

"We are going to do a psychic reading in the car park because Sheila has to get dog food and bags."

"I don't know anything about psychics, but I have to say that doesn't sound like any psychic I've ever heard of," said Juan. "What are you doing with a psychic anyway? Aren't you supposed to be at work?"

"Long story - I saw a sign and thought I'd come and see her."

"A sign? What like a feather floating down or a rainbow suddenly appearing?"

"No - a sign on a noticeboard."

"Right. OK. Not quite as glamorous. Why didn't you tell me? I would have come with you. Are you sure she's not going to kidnap you?"

"I'm fairly sure. Hang on, she's coming back. I'll talk to you later."

I dropped my phone into my lap, and looked out to where Sheila was striding through the car park - her yellow hair dazzling in the afternoon sunshine and her cloak sparkling as if it were covered in diamonds. Her appearance contrasted so vividly with the everyday Asda shoppers all around her, it looked as if she had been beamed down from another planet. She threw the bags into the boot and climbed into the driving seat.

"Where is Merlin?" she asked.

"Who's Merlin?"

"The dog. Derek calls him Tyson, but I call him Merlin when Derek's not around. Where is he?"

I noticed she was holding a dog treat packet in her hand. I followed her gaze to the back seat where there was no sign of the dog.

"Oh my God, I don't know," I said.

"You're supposed to be looking after him."

At this point, I was too worried about the fact that I'd lost her dog to suggest that if she was a real psychic, she might be able to work out where he was. But perhaps that's not how psychics work. We both stared at the empty back seat as if he might somehow materialise out of the worn leather. Then we heard a little squeaking sound, we looked at each other.

"Where is he?" repeated Sheila.

"Well he's definitely here somewhere," I said, rather unhelpfully, but it was the best I could do. Then I looked at my bag, nestling on the floor in front of me. It wriggled a little. Thank God for that.

"He's climbed into my bag, look,"

"Oh darling, Merlin, what are you like?" said Sheila, as I lifted my bag onto my lap and Sheila took her precious pet, feeding him the dog treats and stroking him maniacally.

"Right, let's start this reading. Take Merlin."

I held Merlin while he chewed away on something that smelled like rotting human flesh. Sheila jumped out of the car and went around to the boot, returning with her large bag with stars and moons on it.

"Shall we do tarot first?" she said, sitting back down in the driver's seat.

"Sure." I had no idea, to be honest. I wasn't even sure what there was besides tarot. Tea leaf reading? That didn't seem very practical in the Asda car park. Sheila delved into her large bag and pulled out tarot cards. She also had one of those odd glass ball things in there. She placed Merlin in the bag next to all the psychic stuff and placed it in the back seat.

"I will do your numbers after," she said. "But I think tarot is the best place to start."

I nodded vigorously as she began to shuffle the cards with great dexterity... she was like a magician on a cruise ship. I expected her to produce a card from behind my ear, but I could see she wasn't happy...her painted on eyebrows had sunk so low that they were nearly where they ought to be.

"It's not going to work in the car," she said. "Come with me."

She gathered her bag, complete with Merlin, and led me through the car park and towards the shop. I didn't really want to do tarot reading in the shop itself. That seemed altogether too inappropriate a setting for her to weave her mystical magic and make predictions about the rest of my life, but something stopped me from saying anything. Perhaps it was the way she strode with such confidence and such determination towards the frozen food section, and wiped the top of one of the large freezers with the sleeve of her magnificent gold threaded coat, but I just followed her, blindly

CHAPTER THIRTEEN

Sheila fiddled with her phone and stood it upright, before she laid out the shuffled cards on top of the freezer, putting them face down and spreading them out. I didn't realise what she was doing at the time, but it turned out that she was videoing the whole thing on her phone, so I could look through it afterwards and remind myself of the cards I'd picked, and what they meant.

"Pick three of them," she said, while elderly ladies clutching shopping trolleys paused to watch us. I lifted the cards which I was 'drawn to' (Sheila's words – they all looked the damn same to me) and she studied them carefully.

"Brenda, come and have a look at this," shouted one lady, forcing the others gathered around us to make shhhh... noises to keep her quiet. They didn't want the performance to end.

"Okay, what have we got here," Sheila said, smiling at me. Then she put the card down firmly. I didn't realise quite how many people had gathered around us until I heard a cheer go up.

"We've got the lovers, and it's upright.... well that's a very good start. It looks like love is coming your way, young lady."

I felt myself flush red from the tips of my roots to the soles of my feet: it might have been embarrassment, but it was also huge delight, relief even, that love was coming my way. An image of Ted filled my mind.

Then she placed another card down and told me it was the Empress, a sign of fertility and motherhood. This card builds on the first," she said. "There's definitely a big focus on love in your life."

The next card in the set was the Three of Wands.

"It's reversed," she said, while the assembled crowd oooh-d at this news.

"What does that mean?"

"It means that the love won't be coming instantly. It will be slow."

"But I want it to come now."

"The card is telling us there will be delays and obstacles. But you will get there in the end."

Sheila placed lots of other cards on the freezer, until they covered so much of it that you couldn't see the haddock in parsley sauce and fish fingers inside it.

She told me that my health would improve as I lost weight, that I would get a new job in the next year, and that there would be a surprise guest appearing in the mornings. I knew it was probably rubbish, but I lapped it up. I loved how sure she was and how convinced that this would all come to pass.

"Do you have any red in your life?" she asked.

"I don't know what that means?" I tried.

"I'm just seeing a redness, attached to an important event. It's a redness that you will feel very positive about."

We were causing a considerable amount of interest, but I didn't know quite how much until Sheila laid the next card down and there was a huge intake of breath.

"Keep your enemy close," she said. "You must keep her close."

I scribbled all of this down in the notebook she had given me.

"I don't think I have any enemies," I said. "I mean - who would that be?"

"I don't know. Nothing's dawning on me, but it's what the cards say."

"Supervisor to aisle four, please," came over the tannoy. "Supervisor to aisle four."

"Oh no. That's our cue to leave," said Sheila, sweeping all the cards into her bag, on top of poor Merlin, before heading for the exit. There was a huge groan and lots of questions from the assembled crowd who began to follow us into the car park. There were quite a few questions from me too.

"When you say 'our cue to leave' you make it sound as if you've done this sort of thing before."

"Yes, many times," said Sheila, struggling to get the engine started in her panic to get away. It was like we were on a heist or something.

"Why on earth do you do your readings in Asda?" I asked.

"Have you seen the state of my house?"

I looked at her, and in that minute, all I wanted for Sheila was for her to live in a home that was more welcoming than the frozen fish section at Asda.

We zoomed out of the car park, and onto the main road. "There we are," she said. "That worked out well, didn't it?"

"Uh, yes," I replied. I was slightly shaken, if I'm honest. I was also still digesting everything she had said.

The main points appeared to be: I was going to get back with Ted. That was what mattered the most. But the bad news was that it wasn't going to happen imminently, which meant it probably wasn't going to happen at the party, despite the redness she saw which I apparently thought was swing things in my favour. I had no idea what this meant, but she told me to make a note of it and remember it, so I did and I would.

There was good news in that I would be healthier, and a surprise guest would appear in the mornings. She must have meant Juan, coming to my room with a cup of tea, but I wasn't sure.

What else did she say? Oh yes – a new job. Well that would be great, I really did feel like it was time for me to move on to something more challenging (by that I mean more lucrative).

"All in all, it's good news, isn't it?" I said. "But I also wanted to ask about my family and my friends and find out whether they will be OK. I've got two great friends: Juan and Charlie. I hope they have great futures ahead, and what about my mum and dad?"

"It's all good news, angel," said Sheila warmly. "There was nothing bad in your reading in relation to friends and family: they are going to be fine."

"Oh good," I said.

"You'll get your man but you have to be patient. If he's worth waiting for, then you'll get him."

"And a new job would be fun, And I'm really pleased that I'm going to get healthier. I just want to lose more weight and feel better about myself."

"Yes," she said. "Life's going to come together well for you, my dear. Do remember what I said at the end though, won't you?"

"What was that?"

"Keep your enemies close. You may not think you have any, but swill my words around your mind, play the tape when I send it to you. Stay in touch with my words and you'll work out what they mean."

"Sure," I said, as we pulled up outside her house and she leaned over to give me a kiss. "You know where I am if you need me. Merlin and I will be thinking of you and sending good vibes to you. If you want to come and see me again, I can tell you all about your angel, but leave it awhile, see how things go, but I'm always here if you want to talk anymore."

With that I paid her and climbed out of the car. It has been the most astonishing day, perhaps unique. I didn't know whether anyone else's day had featured a reading in the frozen food section of the big Asda in Sunbury, but I doubted it. I had my notebook with all my scribbles in, and she would send me a voice recording of the reading. Now it was time to get the bus home.

CHAPTER FOURTEEN

I woke up the next morning feeling bright, happy and confident with the world. When I got in last night, Juan and Charlie had listened open-mouthed as I'd explained my day to them, and Juan had cautioned me against turning up at the houses of random psychics without telling anyone. I took his point, but I was still glad I'd gone. My reading with Sheila had given me a positivity that I hadn't felt for ages. If she was right, I was going to win back Ted forever, lose weight and get a new job. The three things in the world that I most wanted to do. Also, my friends and family were all well and no problems were forecast. It was all good news. It sounded like the Ted thing might be a slow burner but, as long as I got there in the end, it was fine. I just had to be patient.

In order to fulfil the weight loss prediction, though, I had to get cracking. I had lost weight on the Italy retreat and my efforts at dieting since returning had led to weight loss that I could feel. My trousers were looser and I could see that my face looked thinner. Now I needed to up the ante. I decided, rather rashly, perhaps, that would consume nothing but juices for the day, and see how I felt by the end.

Annoyingly I didn't have a juicer, but I did have a blender, which was more or less the same thing, so after gathering up a whole load of fruit and vegetables I began chopping it up and chucking it in. Kale, spinach, apple and carrot - how could that lot not be nutritious and delicious? I pressed the button and the whole thing zoomed around, creating a healthy if unpalatable green liquid. The slight problem with having no juicer, was that the fruit and vegetables didn't quite turn into a blended juice; it was more of a half-blended, lumpy mixture. I poured it into two glasses and had a taste... My first mouthful was okay, and I was in the process of mentally complimenting myself on my achievement, when I got a huge mouth of nasty green mash, bits of chewy kale. It was one of my more unpleasant food experiences.

I drank half of it before deciding that it was way too disgusting and tipping it down the sink. It sat in the sink hole like slime, so I had to scoop it out with my fingers and slop it into the bin. The other glass of it I tipped into an airtight container for lunch. If I did this every day, I'd soon lose weight and feel great. I even felt quite full as I left the house and walked down the road to catch the bus.

By the time I reached work, things were different; I felt ravenous. How could that possibly be the case? One bus journey and the green gunk had gone all the way through me. I was starving to the point of madness by about 10 am, but as I pottered around the garden centre, helping customers and organising plants, I chose to ignore the pain scratching at my stomach, and distract myself with the rearranging of all the plants that were perfectly well arranged in the first place. Lunchtime came and I opened my locker...the second bottle of juice sat there, giving me a lurid green smile. This bottle had the added advantage of having sat in my locker all morning so it was not only lumpy but also warm and unpleasant.

I got half way through it and gave up. It was disgusting. I had to throw it away, but I knew that I couldn't buy anything from the cafe to eat: I was banned from the cafe in the store until after the party. It looked like being a long and boring lunch hour, watching as customers strolled around outside from the relative secrecy of the staff room. It would have been much nicer to sit in the cafe, but I couldn't. I wasn't able to sit there without eating; every time I went in there, I put on 20lbs. It was the smells. They did this all-day breakfast ...bacon, toast, sausage and eggs. It threw me into a wild spin. I lost all control. My record was three breakfasts on one day, and I couldn't take any risks with the party coming up.

I pulled out my phone to check for messages and - to my delight - there was the video, emailed over by Sheila. There was no one else in the staff room, so I played it straight away, listening as the sound of Sheila's voice flooded into the room, along with the cacophony created by a dozen or more shoppers gathered around the freezer in the local branch of Asda.

I listened to the whole tape. It was only about 23 minutes long, which surprised me. I felt like I've been in there forever having my fortune read. It made me laugh as I heard the shoppers oooo-ing and ahhh-ing, then the announcement that a supervisor should head for our aisle, and the frantic packing up before the tape stopped. I wrote down the key points. It was all really good news, the only unnerving things were her suggestion that it was going to take a long time to get back with Ted, and the warning at the end: "beware of your enemies."

What on earth did that mean? What enemies? She said it directly after talking about Ted, so the only conclusion I could come to was that she was suggesting that there was an enemy between me and Ted. I played that section of the tape back again. "Keep your enemy close" then when I asked her to be more specific, she said: "nothing's dawning on me."

Dawning? Oh My God. She had to mean Dawn. Blimey.

Did I need to keep Dawn close? It wasn't a thought that appealed a great deal. I wasn't overly fond of the woman at the best of times, and this quite obviously, was not the best of times.

I needed to get closer to her. But, how? I was Facebook stalking her already. What else could I do?

This thought dominated my thinking all afternoon as I struggled to function in a state of complete exhaustion through lack of food and wholehearted distraction through thoughts of Dawn.

I charged the wrong price for a petunia, causing the poor customer to go into near meltdown with my request for £599.99.

"You really think someone is going to pay nearly £600 for that?" she said. Her raised voice caught the attention of Keith, the store manager. "I understand you accidentally putting the wrong price in, but only an idiot could look at it, and think that's right."

I felt like I was going to cry.

"Everything OK?" said Keith, looking at the astronomical price on the till, my pale face, and the angry customer.

"Not really," I said, my lip quivering.

Keith took over at that point, charged the woman £5.99 and wished her a good day. Then he turned to me: "You have spent the day dropping things and messing things up, what is wrong with you?"

"I don't feel well."

"Do you want to take a break?"

"I feel like I'm going to faint," I said, clinging onto the side of the till.

"Oh no. This isn't women's problems again, is it?"

"Yes," I said quickly. "That's right."

I really should stop doing that. It's not good for my feminist credentials to be using my femininity to get out of working.

"Beverly, can you come and take over from Mary here. I think you better get yourself home," he said to me.

"If you really think so," I said. Feminism be damned.

It was 4pm when I left the garden centre, I'd been due to work there till six, so it was a nice slice of time off, and I knew exactly where I was going: to see my enemy. I would walk down Dawn's street, find somewhere to hide, near her flat, and emerge and bump into her if I saw her.

I'd been to her flat before to collect tickets and things before various trips, but I'm not the best at directions, and it took me a long time to find her flat. I looked at it with new eyes now: that's where the witch lived. Had Ted been there? I imagined so. There was a small hedge opposite so slipped behind it and thought about what to do next.

I still didn't feel at all well, as I tucked myself down into the branches. My head was spinning and doing that horrible thing where it throbs behind your ear and feels like a minor electrical shock. It wasn't enough to put me off my mission, but it was certainly bloody annoying. I massaged my head with one hand while keenly watching Dawn's flat. I didn't know why I was there, or what I was looking for, and unless she walked down the street, I had no way of befriending her. But I stayed there all the same, tucked out of sight in the foliage.

There was a light on in her flat but I couldn't see any movement. I didn't know which room was at the front though, so I could have been looking at the bathroom or a spare room. I needed to find out the full layout of her apartment. I went into my phone to look at Zoopla, hoping to see how recently she bought it, then I could look through and see whether the particulars were still on line. I swear to God - I might not know the price of a petunia, but I would be a whizz in the FBI. I'd gone full-scale detective on this one.

I put in her address, and was beginning to scan through the options in there when the worst thing in the world happened, Dawn's door opened and she emerged. Not on her own, but with…. Ted. She was with Ted: my Ted! And they were laughing heartily as they walked off down the path together. How dare they?

My head was swimming as they walked past me. The throbbing became more violent and I felt a wave of nausea crash through me. I was holding my breath to avoid them knowing I was there. Then the nausea got worse; flooding through me as I clung onto the branch next to me, hoping to God I wouldn't fall into their path. I felt tired, hungry, lonely and, more than anything, really sad.

Then the branch cracked and I fell to the floor, still holding onto a small bunch of leaves. Everything was whirring around me as I lay on the mud. Then everything disappeared.

CHAPTER FIFTEEN

HAPTER 15

I was fairly sure that the elderly man leaning over me and breathing his horrible breath into my face was not known to me. He gently prized open my eyes as I came to terms with the fact that I appeared to be lying down in a bush.

"You wake now," he instructed in what sounded like a Polish accent. Why was I in a bush in Poland? What the hell on earth did I drink last night?

"Waking time," he said, still trying to ease my eyes open.

"Who are you?" I finally managed to say. "And why are we in Poland?"

"Not Poland," he said, shaking his head.

I sat up and looked around. It was all familiar, but it wasn't home. Then, slowly, the whole thing came back to me...I was outside Dawn's flat. I'd seen her and Ted together. Oh God. My stomach lurched and turned to the side and was sick all over the ground next to me. My Polish friend looked, gasped and grabbed his phone.

"I need ambulance. A lady very ill. so ill. She make very bright green sick all over floor. Terrible green sick with lumps."

I must have passed out after that, because the rest of my memories are very vague...I think I recall the ambulance coming. Well, I certainly have a memory of lots of voices around me and being lifted onto a stretcher. But it was all so distant. More as if I was watching it happen to someone else rather than being an intrinsic part of it. I only started to come back properly and see things clearly when I was in hospital, wired up to a drip and having my blood pressure taken by a rather aggressive-looking nurse.

"You're fine," she told me. "Just dehydrated. What have you eaten today?"

I tried to take her on a colourful explanation of the diet and the party in 10 days' time, and Ted, but she didn't seem remotely interested in my terrible love life.

"What food have you eaten?"

"No food. Just the kale shakes."

"That explains the lurid green colour. Well, it's not enough food. How long have you been dieting like this?"

"I've been dieting forever. All my life. I don't remember a time when I wasn't on a diet. I mean - there must have been a time when I ate freely, but I only remember being on a diet."

"Well, the diet's not working," she said, harshly. "And the shakes you're making aren't giving you enough nutrition. If you want to lose weight, you need a proper weight loss plan. You should go and see your doctor." She stood up to leave, before turning and adding: "Your friends are coming to collect you."

"You phoned them?"

"No," said the angry nurse. "He did."

I looked to the side, and there sat an elderly man, looking at me with a tight smile on his lips. He held a felt brown hat in his hands which he fingered nervously while nodding.

"I Lech. I find you in bush," he said.

"You were the person who called the ambulance?"

"Yes, I call. I see very green sick, Very bad. I call ambulance."

"And you also called my friends?"

"Yes - you tell me to call. You gave me phone. Here..."

He gave me my back my mobile phone. I had no memory of this

at all. Blimey - that kale was strong stuff.

"Thank you very much. What did you say your name was?"

"I Lech," he repeated. "L-e-c-h. I am from Poland."

"You're very kind. Thank you for looking after me."

He put up his hand as if to say that it was no problem at all.

"My name is Mary Brown. It's very nice to meet you. Do you live near the place where I fell?"

"Somewhere near," he said. "I was walk dog in the area."

"Walk your dog? Where is the dog now?"

Lech undid the top of his jacket and a gorgeous furry face popped out. "This Herbata," he said. "I hide her because they no liking animals in hospital."

"No," I said. "No, they do get funny about things like that. What does Herbata mean? Is it a Polish name?"

"Herbata is Polish for tea. I like very much to have cup of

tea."

"That's a lovely name," I said. Naming your dog after a cup of tea. Excellent naming skills. Herbata was beautiful...a tiny little thing with glorious, expressive eyes and a dark nose set in a pile of pale cream fur. I leaned over to pet him just as a young

nurse came along and Lech quickly zipped up his coat. I pulled my hand away swiftly and - I swear to God - it looked

as if we'd been up to no good.

This nurse was much kinder and gentler than the other rather

miserable one, she checked the machines and sat down next to

us. "There's nothing at all to worry about. You'll be able to leave soon, we just need to check the bloods when they come

back and you can get on your way."

"Why did I collapse?" I asked.

"You just didn't eat or drink enough."

I laughed at this point, and my Polish friend and the nurse looked at me quizzically.

"Sorry, I don't mean to laugh, but no one's ever told me that I

don't eat or drink enough before."

"Well you didn't. It's one thing wanting to lose weight, and quite another starving yourself to death. You know you won't lose weight that way, don't you? Your body will just cling onto every calorie you give it, and make it even harder to lose weight. Come on, get out of bed and let's check something."

I clambered out and she asked me to step onto the scales."

"You are 17st 10lb," said the nurse.

"I'm what?"

"Sorry, has that shocked you? Weren't you expecting it to be that much?"

"No. I'm thrilled. I was 20 stone last time I weighed myself," I said. "I've lost over two stone!"

The nurse smiled. "Well that's good news then. Let me get you a cup of tea and some biscuits while we're waiting for the blood results."

"Can I ask a favour?"

"Sure."

"Can my friend Lech have a cup of tea too? And can we have a LOT of biscuits?"

If Ted was going off on dates with Dawn, and I had landed up

in hospital because of not eating enough, then clearly the

universe was trying to tell me something, and I think that what

it was trying to tell me was that I needed to forget about Ted,

forget about the party and concentrate on enjoying life a

bit...and eating lots of biscuits.

I got out of the bed and sat on the edge, chatting to Lech while

we both drank our tea. He treated me to the occasional peak

inside his jacket (you see how rude this all sounds...but all he

was doing was showing me his dog. Now that sounds rude as

well. I'd like to point out that 'dog' is not a euphemism for

anything, and when I say that a strange man asked me to look inside his clothing and stroke his dog, it was all entirely innocent).

Our next visit was from the angry nurse. We had named her Twardy - Polish for tough. And I had to try very hard not to look at Lech when she strode up to the bed for fear we might

start laughing.

"Back into the bed," she said.

"But I don't think I'm staying. I'm fine. I don't need to be in bed."

"What do you mean you don't think you're staying. Of course

you are. In the bed."

Obediently, I climbed under the covers and looked at Lech who shrugged his shoulders and passed me a biscuit.

"Why have you got so many of those?" she said, seeing the plate teeming with bourbon creams and digestives.

"I was hungry," I said, rather pitifully.

The nurse stormed off to the next bed and dramatically pulled back the curtain that had been shielding the occupant from me. In it lay a woman, I guess she would be in her late 50s. Once the angry nurse had gone, I smiled at the patient and signalled for her to come over and join us for biscuits. She climbed out of bed without revealing any obvious physical ailments, and tiptoed over to us.

"I'm Mary and this is Lech," I said. Her name was Jayne and she was very distressed.

"There's nothing wrong with me," she said. "I came in to visit my husband and the angry nurse told me to get into the bed. Now she won't let me go. If we weren't on the fourth floor I'd have climbed out of the window by now."

"Nothing is wrong with you?" said Lech, incredulous.

"Nothing at all. Every time I try to go, she sends me back to bed.

"Just put your shoes on and leave, they can't make you stay," I said.

"You know, I think I will," she replied, finishing her biscuit, then walking back to her bed and retrieving her shoes. But before she could slip her foot into one, nurse Twardy was back.

"What are you doing out of bed?" she asked.

Jayne jumped straight back beneath the covers, shut her eyes and pretended to be asleep.

"She's never getting out of here," I said to Lech, who had his hand down the front of his jacket and was playing with his dog (again - not a euphemism).

I heard Juan and Charlie before I saw them...the gentle clicking of Charlie's high heels on the polished hospital floor and the sound of Juan chatting away in his lovely, lyrical Spanish accent. Then I saw Jayne in the bed opposite gasp and stare and I knew she could be looking at only one person.

"Juan and Charlie...my heroes," I said, as they appeared before me: Juan dressed in all his finery. Today it was canary yellow trousers with a matching yellow leather jacket. I have no idea where he would even buy this stuff...who would sell it?

"Darling," he trilled as he approached the bed. "We've come to rescue you."

He had a yellow man bag with him which perfectly matched the jacket. "You look like a new-born chick," I said. "The yellow outfit is incredible."

"I bought it today...while you were hurling yourself into bushes, I was in Hoxton. I bought a scarlet PVC mac as well. It only has one sleeve."

"Of course it does," I said.

"Well, come on...let's go."

"I've been told I'm not allowed to go. The grumpy nurse over there made me get back into bed."

"That nurse said you can go," said Juan, sweeping his arm towards the reception area where the nicer nurse sat, drinking from a huge Sports Direct mug. His dramatic pointing revealed jangling gold bangles on his wrist. "She said the blood results are fine and we can take you away whenever you like. Apparently you haven't been eating properly and were dehydrated because you were sick."

I looked over at Lech who was staring at Juan as if he'd never seen anyone quite like him, which he probably hadn't. I don't know how many men you get in banana-yellow, leather jackets in Poland.

"This is Lech. He rescued me."

"Ah," said Charlie, pulling herself away from the resuscitation posters on the wall and joining me at my bedside.

"Hello Lech - it was you who rang me, wasn't it?"

"Yes. I ring," said Lech, pulling his hand out of his jacket and shaking hands with both of them.

"Enchante," said Juan, with what looked like a small curtsy. "Thanks for looking after our girl."

Lech nodded and smiled. "No problem."

"Shall we go?" said Juan

I wasn't at all sure how this would pan out...I had a strong feeling that as soon as I tried to get up, old Angry Pants would be back over.

"Do you live near where Mary collapsed?" Charlie asked. "We can easily drive you home."

"Quite near there," he said. "In next road."

As I put my shoes on, the three of them continued to chat. Out of the corner of my eye I could see Angry Pants coming towards us.

"You're not going anywhere. No one told you that you could go."

"Oh, for heaven's sake, she's quite ready to go," said Juan. "Why on earth would you keep her here?"

We braced ourselves for an onslaught, but the nurse looked at Juan with a tenderness we hadn't witnessed before.

"You remind me of my third husband," she said coyly.

"Third husband?" Juan said. "How many have you had?"

"Two," she replied with a wink.

"Let's go," he said.

"Stay awhile," said the nurse, and I was tempted to ask Juan to stay and distract her while we all escaped, but I think she might have eaten him alive.

"I must take my friend home, but it's been adorable to meet you."

"And you," she said, giving a tiny curtsey.

"Can I come?" shouted Jayne from the next bed, sensing that this was the best moment to escape.

"Of course," I said.

We all trouped out of the hospital. I felt quite heady when I stepped out of bed. I didn't want to tell anyone in case they tried to keep me in, but everything was a big hazy as we all trouped down the corridor. I'd managed to get myself in hospital through the mad dieting and the heart-break of seeing Dawn together. I had to sort myself out.

Charlie put her arm through mine, and there was something about the gesture that gave me a lift, an injection of confidence. I pushed thoughts of Dawn and Ted to the back of my mind, and tried to focus on the fact that I had lost over two stones.

We jumped into Charlie's smart car. Me, a man in a banana yellow leather jacket, Jayne carrying her shoes and an elderly Polish man with a dog inside his jacket. It had been one hell of a day.

CHAPTER SIXTEEN

" $\mathcal{H}$ ow are you feeling now?" asked Charlie, putting a soft blanket over my legs and tucking it under me as I sat on the sofa. In exactly the same way as you would if your elderly grandmother came to visit.

"I'm OK," I said. "I'm so pleased that Lech found me though."

"Yes, I know. That was lucky. What were you doing in the bushes? In fact - no - strike that - what were you doing on Lambourne Street in the first place?"

"It doesn't matter," I said dismally, looking down at my hands in my lap.

"Oh," said Juan. "You are clearly up to something you don't want to tell us about... Is there a new man in your life?"

I looked up and Juan and tilted my head to one side as if to indicate the absolute unlikeliness of the scenario.

"What were you doing there?" Charlie gently stroked my hair as she spoke. They had gone full good cop: bad cop on me.

"If you must know, I was spying on Dawn," I said, and as I said it, I realised how terrible it sounded.

"Not in a bad way...I wasn't going to harm her or anything. It's just...do you remember the psychic I went to see? The one who read my tarot cards in Asda and said all sorts of really nice things to me?"

"Yes," they both replied, cautiously.

"Well she told me to keep my enemy close. I didn't think I had an enemy, so I asked her what she thought this meant and she said 'nothing's dawning on me.' So, I worked out it was Dawn. After work I went and stood outside Dawn's flat and watched her. I was just standing there, beginning to question whether this was a good idea since I didn't even know whether I was looking at the back of the house or the front of the house when I saw Ted and her leave to go on a date, I saw them leaving laughing and smiling and then I collapsed."

"Oh my darling," said Juan leaping from his chair across the room and hurling himself at me, holding me in a tight hug. "I'm so sorry my angel. Why didn't you tell one of us? I'd have come with you. And I would've punched Ted in his stupid fat face."

This aggressive comment from Juan make me smile, which is what he intended, I imagine,

"I can't think of anything funnier than thought of you and Ted in a fight," I said. "He must be twice your size."

"Oh no, I wasn't going to fight him, I was going to punch him and skip away very fast."

It was agreed that punching was not the way forward, but I think they both realised why I had taken it upon myself to stand outside Dawn's flat. One thing we also all agreed on was that, after the shock of seeing Ted and Dawn, followed by the drama of the hospital visit, the only way forward was pizza.

A call to Dominos and a 20-minute wait and the emotional and physical pain (I had terrible bruising on my legs) was about to be soothed by melted mozzarella and lots of deep pan loveliness.

The doorbell went and Juan leaped up to answer it, and greet the kindly man carrying lots of boxes containing delicious pizza.

Closely behind the pizza man came Dave, having seen the arrival of the Dominos driver from his flat, and determined that he too would like to join in the feast. Luckily, we had ordered enough for about 20 people, so there was plenty to go around.

What's up with your leg?" asked Dave. The bruising was already starting to show, and grazes sat angrily along my leg where the skin had been scraped off by branches.

"I was a Dawn stalker," I said. "And it didn't go very well. I turned up at her house and caught her leaving with Ted, collapsed into the bushes, scraping myself to death in the process, and a Polish man called for an ambulance."

"Bloody hell. Tonight?"

"Yep. I was only there for an hour or so, but it was a bit of a miserable end to a horrible day."

Christ," said Dave. "How are you feeling now?"

"A bit light headed and tired," I said. "I'm going to be great after this pizza though."

There was silence after that, as they all shoved way too much pizza into their mouths and completely lost the ability to communicate.

It was Juan who broke the silence.

"Oh, Mary, I forgot to tell you. There was a phone call for you earlier. It was the woman from the hotel in Italy, the weight loss place. I think she said her name was Eva Bianca."

"Oh my God. You mean the owner of the hotel. What did she want?"

" I'm not really sure. When I said 'Juan speaking,' she said 'Ah - you're the guy who was hiding in Mary's room'.

"I didn't know what to say, so I just said sorry, and told her I didn't realise anyone knew that I was there. I explained that I had just come out to support you because you've been through a difficult time.

"She said not to worry, they all found it very amusing that I was hiding whenever anyone came to the room. She said I was the talk of the hotel."

"Oh Christ."

"She also said that she has a gift for you, and you need to be dressed in leisurewear and ready at 7am tomorrow morning."

"What?"

"That's all she said. She made me promise to make sure you were up."

"Right," I said, pushing away the rest of my slice of pizza. I could only eat half a slice; I'd normally have finished the whole pizza by now.

I went to bed early, and set the alarm for 6:45 am, even though I hadn't a clue what to expect at that ungodly hour. I climbed into bed, pulled the covers over me and tried really hard not to cry. Seeing Ted had pulled up so many emotions that I'd tried to bury. Seeing him with Dawn was like a bullet to the heart. I tried to hold back the tears but it was no good. I fell asleep on a soaking wet pillow, feeling sad and alone.

. . .

IT WAS ACTUALLY 6.55 WHEN THE DOORBELL WENT, AND I WAS halfway into a pair of unflattering tracksuit bottoms (are there any other kind. Honestly, unless you look like Jess Ennis, you're doomed to look like a Telly Tubby in them). The doorbell rang for a second time as I finished climbing into them at top speed, threw on a T-shirt and hurtled my way to the front door, desperate to see what my surprise was. Could it be a dog? A food parcel? But why the need for leisure clothing? I heard the door of Juan's bedroom open behind me. He must have set his alarm as well, just to see what was going on. I swung the front door open to see a well-built man in tight t-shirt and shorts. He was very muscular, like a rugby player, and looked as if he had to come for a fight or something, all stubbly and veiny. If this was my morning present, things were really looking up.

"Are you Mary?" he asked.

"Yes," I said cautiously. Was he a strippergram? Or had he come to help me with household chores? With my luck, it would be the latter.

" My name is Guillaume and I'm your fitness trainer. I've been told that you've got a big party to go to on Saturday, so I have been sent by Eva to make sure you're in the best possible shape. I'll be coming three times this week, and we're going to get you looking even more fabulous than you do now."

I heard Juan run back into his room and I heard the door slam. I assumed he wanted no part of early-morning fitness sessions. To be honest, I wished I could do the same.

"Can I come in?"

"Of course, Guillaume."

"Please - call me Gilly," he said. He had a ridiculously deep voice and what sounded like a slight South African accent.

I stood back and allowed him and his massive sports bag

inside. I peered into the bag as he walked past me...I could see some sort of ball and a mat in it, a notebook and various other paraphernalia. I let him into the sitting room, and he sat down on the sofa.

"Right then, we are going to do a general fitness workout three times this week to give you an idea of lots of different things you can do on your own in the future.

Gilly proceeded to measure me, weigh me, and do tests to establish how strong I was, how flexible and what my heart rate was. He had me touching my toes stretching out and seeing how many press ups and sit-ups I could do in a minute. He made furious notes on his notebook while I performed.

"Right, now let's go outside and do some training."

"Are you for real?" I asked. "Wasn't that the training? I'm exhausted already."

"Ha, ha, very funny," he said, walking towards the door.

Ladies and gentlemen, I wasn't being funny; I did genuinely think that was the exercise session and I was bloody glad that it was all over. Now he was expecting me to do a whole other session.

"Come on, exercise time."

"Can I come too?" said a voice from the doorway. It was Juan. His rush back into his room earlier hadn't been because he didn't want to come out with us, it was because he did want to come out with us and was heading back to get himself dressed in his gym kit. Alas, his idea of gym kit was like no one else's in the world's idea of gym kit. He had on sparkly red leggings that must have come from the days when he was a dancer on a cruise ship. On top he had a little white T-shirt, with a black leather jacket slung over his shoulders.

"You look like you're going to star in Grease the musical, not walk through the streets of Cobham."

"These are the only leggings I have," he said innocently, while staring at Gilly. He was lying. I'd seen him go to his Pilates classes in lots of different leggings, and none of them had red sequins on.

"Fine by me. I'm Gilly, by the way."

My fitness trainer put out his hand and Juan put out his and their eyes locked, and I swear there was some sort of flicker of interest between them. I don't know how, because Gilly didn't look at all gay, while Juan looked like the gayest man in the world.

"After you, my lady," said Gilly. I looked up assuming he was talking to me, but realised he was looking straight at my lovely gay friend. Juan wiggled his way through the door, while Gilly didn't take his eyes off him once. Well this was going to be interesting.

CHAPTER SEVENTEEN

$\mathcal{F}$or the first session we agreed to concentrate on some light aerobic work. The only problem was that Gilly and I had quite different views about what constituted 'light.'

"Come on," he said, handing me some fairly hefty weights. "Let's go power walking, then we can get really stuck in."

As far as I was concerned, power walking WAS getting really stuck in, especially when you were carrying very heavy weights. But I was determined not to complain all the time. This was a really kind gesture from Eva, and I needed to give it all I had. So, with that in mind, I bucked up my ideas, and the three of us strode at speed through the streets of Cobham, swinging our arms in the early morning air and breathing deeply, as Gilly upped the pace until all three of us were almost running.

"How long have you been doing this for?" I asked Gilly when I finally caught up with him.

"For about 10 years," he said. He explained that he went straight into personal training after school.

Every time Gilly spoke, even to say the dullest, most anodyne things, Juan would say: "Oooo, that's interesting" and "Aren't you clever" like a hopeless teenager who'd fallen in love with her teacher. Gilly said he had spent a period of time out in Italy, working at the Bianca hotel group, but for the rest of the time had been working for himself, mainly with bored, stay at home mums, who were determined to look absolutely perfect.

"Wow, Gilly. Amazing," said Juan. Seriously, I needed to have a word with him when we got home.

"The perfect mums are all hangry and not a lot of fun," he said. "Exercise should be something lovely in your day, wanting to look good should be something that empowers you. These women have such low self-esteem, it's as if they exist to look good. I'm really not a big fan of getting yourself into such a state about the way you look that it stops you doing things if you don't feel perfect. That can't be a good way to live."

"I think you're wrong," I said, jokingly. "I treat my body like a temple and would be horrified if it was ever less than perfect." I smiled at Juan whose eyes didn't return my gaze because they were so focused on Gilly's bottom. Gilly, meanwhile, looked at me and smiled.

"Of course, I didn't mean to cause offence."

"No. You big daft fool, I'm only joking with you," I said. "Look at the state of me...do I look as if I treat my body as if it were a holy temple? I spend more time eating pizza than I spend doing sit ups. Just joshing with you."

Gilly laughed and gave me a hug. "As it happens, I think a body that looked like a temple would be very unattractive, wouldn't it? Let's just teach you some tips for being as healthy as possible, and that's all you need to incorporate into your life. I know we've only got three sessions, but that will be enough to give you a real insight into exercising at home, and will definitely make you feel a bit better for that party on Saturday. Okay?"

Thoughts of the party made me feel anything but okay following yesterday's sighting. It was obvious that Ted was going to bring Dawn with him, and I honestly didn't think I could bear it. In fact, there was a huge part of me that wanted to disappear to mum and dad's for the weekend, and not have anything to do with the party. If it weren't for the fact that Charlie was such an amazing, brilliant friend to me, and I wanted to see her on her special day, I wouldn't be anywhere near the place.

"Are you ready for a little jog?" said Gilly.

"I've never felt less ready for anything in my life."

"Just to that lamppost," he said, heading off on a light jog. I ran beside him, feeling myself wibble and wobble inside my T-shirt. I could hear Juan rustling as he jogged beside me, and I realised it was the sequins rubbing between his legs, it made me laugh out loud. We were quite a comical threesome really, when you thought about it.

At the lamppost we were allowed to walk again, so we strolled into a small park, then it was time to run again...we sped passed a children's play area with swings, a roundabout and a slide, and for one delightful moment I thought we might be going into play on them. But, no, of course we weren't. Gilly kept marching right past the kids play area to a large stretch of grass. He put down his bag and took two cones out. Suddenly this felt like no fun at all. Everyone knows that cones spell trouble. It's the first rule of PE.

"Okay, Juan you come and stand on this cone and Mary on that cone." The cones were about 100m from one another and Gilly explained that he wanted us to run towards one another and give each other a high-five in the middle and then run on.

"Now skip back, and when you meet in the middle run round around each other three times."

This is how the session continued, lots of running, skipping, dancing sideways, running backwards, doing jumping jacks and generally wearing myself out so much I thought I might die.

"Just before we finish, I'd like you both to skip around the park," said Gilly, handing us a skipping rope each. Because it was the last thing in the session, I headed off quickly, swinging my rope with glee, and making it halfway round before I looked back and saw Juan stumbling like a fool as he attempted to follow me.

"I've never skipped before," he said.

"What? Never?"

"I went to a boys' boarding school darling, there wasn't much call for skipping."

I got back to Gilly and received a high five for all my efforts, before we stretched out every muscle in my poor, weary body.

I want you to go home and write down in a notebook everything we've done today, okay?" said Gilly. "Then if, in the future, you find yourself having a spare 10 minutes or 15 minutes you can pull out your notebook and just do some of the things we've done today. Write them down when you get home, and I'll see you on Wednesday."

I thanked Gilly, Juan waved at him coquettishly, and we both headed back to my flat.

"You are soooo going to end up in bed with that man," I said.

Juan high-fived me and we walked back in silence, almost dead on our feet.

That night I emailed Eva to thank her for the gift and told her how much I'd enjoyed the session (yes, I lied to her).

CHAPTER EIGHTEEN

*W*ednesday seemed to come around with staggering speed, and before the aches and pains from the Monday session had even begun to subside, it was 7am and Gilly was already at the door. This time he had no bag with him, which I took to be a good thing...it was all the cone related activity last time that had left me on my knees with exhaustion. Surely no cones meant no agony?

"Today we're going to go to my gym for a workout," he said. And in that split second, I realised that cones might be the least of my worries.

We followed Gilly at an incredible pace. I was forced to do little skips to catch up every so often, until we got to a gym I had never noticed before. It was called Riverside Gym and though quite small from the outside, it still seemed to contain all the horrific equipment that one would expect from such an establishment.

"I don't like gyms," I said. I sounded a bit like a petulant schoolgirl, which was an accurate reflection of exactly how I was feeling. Both walls of the gym were covered in mirrors, with changing rooms at the end. The gym itself was about the size of the downstairs of an average house. There were rowing machines, bikes and treadmills to the right and a whole load of weights and ropes and other horrible looking equipment to the left.

"You'll learn to love them, don't worry," said Gilly unconvincingly. We stretched out first, then Gilly led us over to the huge stacks of weights.

"How are you feeling today then...Weak like flower or strong like bull?"

I obviously went for the flower option, so he handed me a weight which to him was, I guess, quite light. It was anything of the kind. With one in each hand, Juan and I were told to face the mirror and do a range of activities: biceps curls, holding our arms out in front of us for a horribly long time, squats, lunges and then more arm exercises.

"I'm just going to get the next equipment ready, have a drink of water," he said.

Juan took a water bottle out of his bag and took a mouthful. Of course, I hadn't thought to bring one with me.

"Here, have mine," he said, handing me the bottle.

"Thanks, I'm dying of thirst."

I put the water bottle to my mouth and sucked on it but nothing came out. I tried again, but still nothing seemed to come out of the bottle, so I squeezed it at the base as I held it to my lips and suddenly a fountain of water shot out of it and completely soaked me.

"What are you doing?" asked Juan.

"I can't work it." I replied as water ran down my face. Juan adjusted it and gave it back to me. "Don't squeeze, just suck," he said, as Gilly returned.

"Good tip," said the personal trainer, winking at Gilly. "Christ, Mary, why are you soaking wet?"

"I couldn't work the water bottle," I replied with a shrug. "It's more complicated than it looks."

"Come on - let's do some ball work." Gilly handed me a ridiculously heavy ball which I was to throw against the wall. It involved a lot of strength to get the thing to reach the wall and a lot of skill to catch it without breaking my fingers.

Next it was Juan's turn. I saw the look of horror on his face as he took the ball from me and felt its weight. He threw the ball against the wall without enough force, so that it rolled down the wall and dropped onto the floor.

"Faster, more forceful," said Gilly, winking at Juan, and I swear to God, it felt like I was in the middle of Carry on Gyming or something.

Gilly hurled the ball at the wall, but it hit the corner, bounced off at a peculiar angle and hit the trampette at some speed. We all watched as it bounced back at us, hitting Gilly firmly in the face.

It was difficult to know whether to laugh or cry, so I opted for laughing.

"Darling I'm sorry. Come here," said Juan, hugging Gilly closely. They seemed to stay in the tight embrace for an unnecessary length of time.

Eventually they pulled apart. "Do you fancy breakfast after Friday's session?" asked Juan.

"Oooo yes, that sounds fun," I replied.

"I was asking Gilly," said Juan.

"Oh, can't I come too?"

"No," said Juan and Gilly in unison. It sounded very much like a date was on the cards.

FRIDAY'S SESSION WAS BACK TO POWER WALKING. GILLY explained that he didn't want to exhaust me or leave me aching for my party the next day, so he proposed a stride through the streets of Cobham, then a relaxing stretch back at the gym. I must confess I gave a sigh of relief at this news. I really didn't want to be beasted again, or throw 20 stone balls at a wall. So, we strolled through the streets, Juan and Gilly powering ahead while I waddled along behind doing my little skips every off so often to keep up with them.

It was a beautiful, clear morning. The one part of these sessions that I had enjoyed (other than watching Gilly and Juan flirt with one another) was seeing the day before going to work. I usually set my alarm to wake up exactly at the time I needed to, in order to make it to work on time. Getting up earlier and doing something constructive before going to work made the whole day better...it made it feel like there was more of a balance between work and home life. I didn't just get up to go to work; I had other things in my day. Work was a part of the day rather than the whole thing...it fit in after exercising and before seeing my friends.

"Here we go," said Gilly as we arrived at the gym for our stretching. Gilly laid me down and stretched my legs for me, pushing my leg up as I lay on the mat. It hurt a lot, of course, because everything in the gym always does, but it was also quite a nice sort of hurt. I felt properly refreshed afterwards.

"Now you need to stretch out your upper body. Just lean against something and push your shoulders forward to really get into the muscle," he suggested.

I walked over to the pile of benches near some cardio equipment, and grabbed onto the top one to stretch my shoulders out. I pushed forwards, entirely unaware that the benches were piled up but not in any way tied down. The bench slid forwards, straight into a row of eight of the blow-up balls that rolled into a stack of foam bricks that yoga people use. The bricks tumbled off their racks onto a guy doing sit ups beneath them.

"Shall we leave it there," said Gilly, after helping the man to his feet and dusting him down, while Juan and I heaped the foam bricks back onto their rack.

I agreed that - yes - it felt very much like the right time to call it a day.

I walked out with Gilly and Juan, but not home with them because they, of course, were off to their breakfast date. I was off to work...to make sure there were house plants aplenty for the good people of Surrey. This evening I would spend time with Charlie, chatting and planning and giggling over the fact that she was going to be 30. How could she be 30? We both still acted like we were about 17, it seemed astonishing that we'd managed to survive our teens and duck and dive our way through our 20s, and now - here we were - facing our 30s.

I knew her party would be great fun. I would make sure she had a good time. As for me...well, a lot of it was out of my control: what would be would be. I would do everything I could to win Ted back, but if he turned up with Dawn, I would just be as polite as possible to them. I would make sure that by the time he left we'd smiled together and laughed together. Fate would do the rest.

"A penny for them?" said Gilly coming over to me.

"Sorry. I was miles away."

"Where were you?"

"I was just thinking about the party tomorrow night, and this guy I really like."

"Look, I hope everything works out for you," he said "If it doesn't, there are loads more guys around. I know you'll find someone wonderful."

Then they left. I watched as they walked off together...Juan with his wiggling bottom and Gilly with his thunder thighs. I really hoped things worked out for them too. I hoped things worked out for everyone.

For now, though, I had to go to work, then I had to pick up the cake I'd ordered and hide it in my flat and I had to wrap the gorgeous handbag we'd bought in Italy.

Tomorrow was the first day of the rest of my life...heaven knows what joys and sorrows it would bring.

ENDS

IT'S PARTY-TIME! ON 1ST JULY WE WILL FIND OUT WHAT HAPPENS at the party, and whether Mary gets her man.

Just click on 'my book' below, and the book will be beamed to you as soon as it is released...like magic.

My Book

WHAT WILL HAPPEN ON JUAN'S DATE?

How will the party go?

Will she come face-to-face with Dawn?

Most importantly…will she get back with Ted.

The book features more from Sheila the Healer, a narrow boat, Juan in a brave rescue attempt, lots from Ted, lots from Mary and a glamorous arrival from Italy…it also features a wonderful love story: but is it the story of Mary and Ted? Or another couple entirely?

My Book

.   .   .

FOR ALL OF BERNICE BLOOM'S BOOKS, SEE:

HTTPS://WWW.AMAZON.CO.UK/KINDLE-STORE-BERNICE-BLOOM/
S?RH=N%3A341677031%2CP_27%3ABERNICE+BLOOM

THANK YOU XXXX

Printed by Amazon Italia Logistica S.r.l.
Torrazza Piemonte (TO), Italy

12973743R00075